The Pregnant Amish Nanny

Expectant Amish Widows Book 6

Samantha Price

Chapter 1

The thief comes only to steal and kill and destroy;
I have come that they may have life,
and have it to the full.
John 10:10

A aron heaved a sigh of relief as he sank into the couch after all his nightly chores were finished. His three children were in bed relatively early in the evening—hopefully they'd remain there. It hadn't been easy coping after his wife's death a year ago, but Aaron had done his best. He couldn't keep relying on his sister-in-law, Heather, to help him. She and his brother, James, had three young children themselves.

Taking a step in faith that he'd be able to find a suitable nanny, Aaron with the help of James, had built a small cabin near his house. Someone had to watch the children while he was at work, and a nanny would also be able to keep the house, tend the animals, and cook the meals. Since Aaron worked from dawn to dusk in the fields, he simply didn't have the time to do all those things himself.

As soon as the cabin had been built, he'd picked up pen and paper and written to his Aunty Bessie who lived in a large community within Lancaster County. He'd been writing to Bessie often since Ellen died and he thought that Bessie would know of a suitable woman who would be able to work for him. Hopefully the unopened letter before him— that he'd received that very day—was telling him that a suitable woman had been found.

Now that he had a quiet moment, he settled back and picked up the letter that he'd been too nervous to open earlier.

Aunty Bessie was the kind of person who knew everyone's business. If Bessie couldn't find him a nanny, then no one could.

Please Gott, may this be a positive response. The worst reply he could think of was that she'd say that there was no one who was willing to travel the long distance north to live in the remote part of the country where he and his brother had moved—

Giles County—as part of a fledgling community.

* * *

Courtney opened the front door to Bessie—a kindly elderly lady who'd befriended her since her recent arrival to the community. The Yoders had been kind enough to allow Courtney to stay with them until she found something more permanent. The Yoders' house was next door to Bessie's.

"Come in, Bessie. I'm afraid Peter and Wilma aren't here right now."

Bessie stepped through the doorway. "It's you I've come to see."

"Oh good."

Bessie was already making her way to the living room so Courtney hurried to catch up. After Bessie sat heavily on the couch, Courtney sat down next to her.

"Can I offer you any tea or *kaffe* perhaps?"

"*Nee,* I just had a cup before I left home. I have some exciting news and I do hope you think it'll be a suitable arrangement for you."

"You've found me a place to stay?" Courtney was aware that the old lady knew everyone in the community and most of the people in the other Amish communities close by.

"I have. My nephew is looking for a nanny to look after his three young *kinner*. He lives a day's journey away, in a small community with only a few families. It's a farming community."

"Is he widowed?"

"*Jah,* I didn't mention that, did I? He's widowed. Ellen died over a year ago now and he's found it difficult to look after the three of them and do all his work."

"He's never had a nanny before?"

Bessie shook her head. "He's never been able to find anyone. I don't know why I didn't think of you before. You'd be perfect. He tells me he's already built a cabin right next to his *haus* ready for a suitable nanny. He's been praying for one for some time."

"That sounds like it would be perfect. I'd be

working for my keep and I love children."

"You'd be paid too, of course, you wouldn't just be working for your board and lodgings. You're good with children; I've noticed that children always flock to you. I told Aaron, my nephew, the very same thing."

"You've spoken to him about me?"

"I hope that's all right, isn't it? You and Wilma told me you need somewhere to live and you need a job—this is perfect for you."

"I do. It hasn't been easy for me since Mark died."

"I still don't think it's right, what his family did to you."

Courtney nodded. Neither did she think it was fair but she wouldn't dwell on it. Mark's *familye* were *Englischers* and had never approved of his choice to join the community—they'd blamed Courtney for his decision. For some reason Mark had bought their *haus* within his family's trust and when he'd died she had no rights to it. Courtney hadn't known how he'd bought the house until after his death. Perhaps it was the only way he could've purchased a house, or maybe he was still holding on to his *Englisch* roots and the *familye* he'd told Courtney he had parted ways with. Courtney would never know the truth of his motives, but she did know that soon after he died she was homeless and penniless.

"What his family did to me is in the past." She shrugged her shoulders and Bessie patted her on her knee.

"Never mind, dear. I got a letter today from Aaron and that prompted me to think of you so of course I wrote back to him right away. I knew you wouldn't mind. Have I done the wrong thing? Should I have talked with you first?"

Courtney laughed. *"Nee.* It sounds perfect for me. I need somewhere quiet and having children to care for suits me perfectly."

"They have become a handful he tells me. They're lively."

"That's *gut.* That means they're healthy. When can I start?"

Bessie laughed. "He'll want you there as soon as possible I'd dare say. He asked me to find someone older. He knew I'd want to match him with a younger woman who'd want to marry him if the decision were left entirely in my hands. Someone like you would be much more suitable."

If she hadn't already felt old and unattractive, Bessie's comment would've made her feel just that way. Courtney was approaching thirty, which seemed old when the typical Amish woman starts looking for a husband well before her eighteenth birthday. She hadn't been lucky in love. The two relationships she had before she met Mark hadn't lasted long and had both ended when the men she was dating opted for prettier more vivacious women. Mark had come along to an Amish wedding when one of his friends had converted and married an Amish woman. It was at the wedding that Courtney first met him.

"I'm glad you think I'll be suitable. That would be something I'd really enjoy. Do you think he'll want to speak to me first?"

"*Nee*. He trusts my judgment. I did take the liberty of saying that you'd take the job."

"You did?"

Bessie nodded and smiled.

"That's *gut*. I suppose that means I'll get there sooner. Can you tell me a little about the *familye?*"

"He grew up here in this community, but his wife, Ellen, didn't. After they met, they moved away shortly after they married, as did his *bruder's familye*. They haven't been back since, and I've never even met his *kinner*. He wrote to me infrequently over the years, but since Ellen died, he's been writing once a week."

Although Courtney wondered how his wife died, she didn't like to ask.

Bessie held her hand over her heart and winced.

Courtney jumped up. "Bessie, are you okay?"

With a furrowed brow Bessie looked up at Courtney and her lips tugged at the corners as though she were trying to make the effort to smile. "It's heartburn, that's all. I'm not having a heart attack or anything."

8

"Are you sure you're all right?"

Bessie nodded. "I had sauerkraut with the evening meal last night. It always gives me pangs of heartburn the next day."

"Have you been to a doctor?"

"Humph! Doctor Schmokter! I don't believe in 'em. I refuse to go running off to a doctor at the first sign of a sniffle or a pain." She stared deeply into Courtney's eyes. "Now don't you worry about me; you look after yourself. I know it's not easy with your husband gone."

Courtney sat down again next to her. "It's been dreadful and lonely."

"It took me some time to adjust to my Alfie being gone, but I'd expected it since his health had gone downhill."

"It would've been nice to have met him. You've told me so many nice things about Alfie."

"Memories are what we have left of them. Memories and the hope that we'll see them again one day as long as we stay on the narrow path right where *Gott* wants us to be."

9

Courtney nodded. She had no intention of going off the path and that's why she'd put the bitter feelings toward her late husband's family aside. A root of bitterness could eat away at a person's soul. His family had tossed her out of her own home because it was in the name of their family trust of which she was not a part. She had soon found out that Mark held no money in his own name, either.

After Mark's death, Courtney was alone and penniless and that's not what Mark would've wanted, but dollar signs was all his family could see. They'd told her that the Amish community should look after her. She couldn't bring herself to tell them about the child she was carrying—the child that would be a part of their family. Of course, one day her child might wish to meet them and she would not stop that from happening. But right now, she had to think of her future, and her baby's, and do what was best. That meant having a home and an income.

"I must go. I just wanted to pop over and see if I hadn't made a mistake by telling him you'd take the job." Bessie stood up. "Why don't you come by tomorrow and I'll tell you as much about them as I know. That'll prepare you for meeting them."

Courtney stood as well. "The children are only young?"

"Jah, from memory, the youngest one is three or so, and the oldest one, Jared, is around eight."

"Such fun ages." She walked Bessie to the door. *"Denke,* Bessie, I appreciate this so much. It sounds like it would suit me well. Are you certain you're okay? You can stay and rest awhile."

"I'm fine. It seems that all the food I like disagrees with me. I'll have to learn to live with bread and broth."

"You might have to if everything else causes you such pain."

"Sauerkraut's the worst."

"You must stop eating it."

Bessie's mouth turned down at the corners. "I will. Every time I eat it, I do it hoping that this will be the time it causes me no ill effects."

"You'll have to be strong. You can't go around

in such pain. Has it gone now?"

She placed her hand over her heart. "It's still there a little, but don't you worry about me. The sooner I go home to be with *Gott,* the sooner I'll see Alfie." Without waiting for Courtney to respond, she said, "*Gut!* See you tomorrow, then?"

Courtney nodded and then watched Bessie walk away. Bessie glanced back at her and waved. Courtney waved back, and when Bessie was out of sight, she closed the door and leaned against it. She felt bad about keeping the fact that she was pregnant from Bessie, but would Bessie think she'd be so suitable working for her nephew had she known? Courtney placed a hand softy on her carefully hidden baby bump. If the community she'd only just arrived in knew of her condition they would've helped her and found her somewhere to live, but she wanted a life of her own and independence. Mark would've wanted Courtney to teach their child the importance of being independent and working hard to give to those in need. One thing Courtney did not want was to be one of those who was in need.

Bessie's visit was an answer to prayer. She'd prayed every night for the perfect place to stay and for the perfect work.

That night, Courtney told Wilma and Peter that she'd soon be leaving and that Bessie had found her a job. Wilma and Peter told her all about Aaron and his brother James, and how they moved to Giles County. She heard that Aaron's wife, Ellen, had drowned in the creek on their property when it was flooding, leaving behind their three young children.

Courtney couldn't wait to get to Bessie's house the next day to hear more about the family she would be working for.

Chapter 2

Do not conform any longer to the pattern of this world,
but be transformed by the renewing of your mind.
Then you will be able to test and approve what
God's will is—his good, pleasing and perfect will.
Romans 12:2

"Aaron is such a lovely boy." Bessie sifted and sorted through a box of letters.

Courtney sat on Bessie's couch wondering if all those letters were from Aaron. "You certainly seem fond of him. You call him a 'boy;' how old did you say he was?"

"He's around thirty. Oh my, I still see him as he was before they moved away, so young he looked then, almost ten years ago." Bessie picked up another letter and studied it. "Ah, now listen to this. *'My heart aches so much for Ellen. I knew I loved her but I never knew how much our hearts and minds were entwined until she was gone. Being without her is like being without my very soul. I*

15

walk around and go about my work every day as half a person. The only reason I have to get out of bed and keep going is our kinner. They must learn how wonderful their mother was and I want to tell them about her, but it pains my heart to speak to them about her. I can't speak of their mother to them without tears coming to my eyes and I don't want them to see their father cry. They carry their own pain of her absence.' And it goes on. I'm the only one he can confide in. He told me that."

Courtney sat listening and wondered if Aaron had any idea that Bessie was reading his letters aloud to people.

"Does that tell you how caring he is?" Bessie asked leaning forward.

"Jah, it does and I know how he feels."

"You and me both. Alfie is the first thing on my mind when I wake up and the last when I go to sleep. Aaron is just devastated about Ellen's death. Here's another one." She lifted another letter out of the pile. *"The one thing I'm happy about is that Ellen always knew how much I loved her and*

16

she loved me the same. We had a truly wonderful double-handful of years together and I thank the Lord daily for His blessings. I know He only gives us what we can bear and I'm hoping my suffering will soon come to an end. You tell me I'll feel better as more time passes and I hope that is true. I long to go to my heavenly home and be with Ellen."

Courtney raised her hand to have her stop reading. "That's truly lovely, but you don't have to read them to me."

Bessie's jaw dropped open. "I need you to see the real Aaron."

"I do, I see the real Aaron. He's heartbroken over losing his *fraa* who he loved so deeply. *"

"So you see what kind of man he is?"

Courtney nodded. *"Jah,* I do. A man still very much in love."

"It's rather sad. It's almost better to have never loved anyone than to love someone-to know real love—and then to lose it." Bessie looked up at her. *"Ach,* I'm sorry, my dear, I didn't think what I was saying. You'd feel the same way, wouldn't you?"

"I do, but most of the time I try not to think about Mark because it's difficult. I'm sure Aaron's *kinner* are a help to him."

"They will be when they're older. Right now he's finding it difficult to be both a *mudder* and *vadder* to the three of them."

"It sounds like it would be perfect for me to go there and help him."

"*Jah*, it does, and he says he doesn't want to marry again and wants a woman who won't stay for a small amount of time. He wants someone who can stay on forever—the right person that is."

"I *am* that person."

"Do you think it might be too isolated for you? It's not a big community like we have here."

'I'm certain it will be perfect. What I need is a quieter life at the moment and to be kept busy, so this job seems like it will suit me just fine."

"Well, I think you'd be perfect. And you two might be a comfort to each other since you've each lost a spouse."

"*Jah*, there's that too. Although I don't think

either of us will feel like discussing it."

"*Nee,* you wouldn't have to. Just to know that someone understands is often all that we need." Bessie smiled kindly and Courtney smiled back. "Shall I write back and tell him I've found someone?"

"*Ach, jah,* please do. I thought you said you already did that."

Bessie looked into the distance. "Did I say that?"

"You said yesterday that you wrote back to him and you told him I'd take the job."

"I can't quite recall that I did." Bessie shook her head. 'It won't matter if I write again."

Courtney considered that Bessie writing twice was better than thinking she'd written and not writing at all. "I'm so excited to start a new life," Courtney said.

"I do hope you like it, but if you don't, he can't force you to stay."

"I'll be fine. Everything you've told me about Aaron and the place he's prepared for a nanny sounds like it will suit me down to the ground."

"I'll send a letter to him today." Bessie clasped both hands to her ample chest. "I can see him right now when he opens the letter. He'll be so pleased." She looked back at Courtney. "Now we have to see how we're going to get you there. Aaron mentioned a bus so there must be a bus. I'll have Milton find out for you." Milton was one of Bessie's sons who lived nearby.

"Denke."

"The community is made up of only five families. The bishop is Eli, a friend who'd grown up with Aaron and his brother, James. They all moved there because reasonably priced farming land is scarce."

"Jah I know. The price of the land keeps going up."

"And it's disappearing fast. That's why some people in our community have had to move away from farming altogether—they simply can't afford the land."

Chapter 3

Trust in the Lord with all your heart
and lean not on your own understanding.
Proverbs 3:5

Aaron ripped open the letter from his Aunty Bessie. So much was at stake, and if there was no lady prepared to work for him, he didn't know what his next step would be. The children were getting more and more difficult to handle with each passing day.

My Dearest Aaron,

I received your letter and have taken a great deal of time to ponder on the question you asked. Do I know anyone who would be suitable to look after your three children now that they don't have a mother?

Had you not expressed your firm desire never to marry, I would have had several young ladies in mind with a view to marriage.

Do I know an older lady who would be prepared to stay in the cabin close to the house that you've prepared, a woman to do all the duties you mentioned?

I know a woman who does not have marriage on her mind, and she is an older woman. Her name is Courtney Lewis, and she is a childless widow. She is of good character, and well respected by all in the community. Since she has nowhere to live, she has been staying with Wilma and Peter Yoder. Wilma tells me that Courtney is hardworking and insists on doing all the chores. Courtney is kind, and of an even temperament. This arrangement would suit Courtney as much as it would suit you.

I took the liberty of talking to Courtney about moving to Giles County and working for you. She is willing to make the move even though I shared with her how you'd explained the area to me in your letters. Please reply with haste.

Yours in the Lord,

Bessie

Aaron felt a load spring off his shoulders. Finally, he was going to have some relief from doing everything himself. He fully understood now how hard it had been for his late wife, Ellen, to look after the three young children, do all the cooking, and keep the house spotless.

His aunt had done a great job finding someone to mind the children and keep the house. He was right in telling her that he wasn't interested in marrying again—he didn't want the distraction of trying to keep a woman happy—a woman who could possibly draw his attention away from his children. He knew if he hadn't stated that bluntly to his aunt in his letters, and told her how in love he'd been with Ellen, she would've tried to find him a wife and not a nanny. He hoped he'd done enough in his letters to convince her of that.

He closed his eyes and pictured this Courtney Lewis that Aunt Bessie had spoken of in her letters. A kindly older woman with a pleasant face, someone who loved children, appeared in his mind's eye.

Denke, Gott.

He picked up pen and paper to send a response, which he'd then take to the post office the very next day. He had to tell his aunt that he'd accept Courtney Lewis since she met with Bessie's approval.

Dear Aunty Bessie,

I hope you remain in good health.

Your letter came as an answer to prayer. I'm in desperate need of a woman like Courtney Lewis. I thank you for finding her for me. She is a blessing and an answer to prayer. I've enclosed money for her fare to Giles County. If you let me know the time she'll arrive, I'll meet her at the bus station.

One day, I hope you'll be able to make the journey to look at the progress we've made here in our small community.

Give my love to all there,

Your nephew,

Aaron

Aaron jumped to his feet and took an envelope out of the drawer, folded the letter in two and popped it into the envelope. He wasn't much of a letter writer but had found an outlet for his emotions as Aunt Bessie encouraged him to share his feelings. After propping the letter on the table by the door so he wouldn't forget it the next day, he headed to the end of the house to look at his sleeping children.

His three children each had their own rooms, but often all slept in the large bed in Jared's room. Jared was the oldest at eight, Ben was six and Amy had just turned four. It was funny to see them sleeping sweetly and quietly when through the day they were rarely still or quiet. Aaron hoped that Courtney was experienced in dealing with lively children like his. He leaned down and kissed each one of them on their foreheads, risking that one of them might wake. Jared was the only one who stirred when his father kissed him. He half-opened his eyes and then promptly closed them.

It had been hard for his children to adjust to

their mother suddenly being gone. Ellen, his wife, had been gone for nearly a year. She'd died while trying to save a calf from drowning in a creek that was flooding. She and the children had been in the house when the rain had been pouring down, and the bleating of a calf caused Ellen to see what was wrong. She'd ordered the children to stay in the house and not come out. When she didn't return, they went to find her. They saw her struggling in the creek pushing and pulling a calf up an embankment.

As soon as she saw them she grew angry and told them, they must go back to the house out of the rain and stay warm.

Jared had grabbed a hand of each of his younger siblings, and they ran back to the house. When their mother didn't come home after some time, they knew something was wrong. Aaron arrived home not long after to find them huddled together in tears. He ran to the bank, but she was nowhere to be seen. She was found a day later—downstream.

As soon as Courtney arrived, life would get

easier, and the pressure would be off his sister-in-law, Heather, who had taken on a huge share of extra work.

Chapter 4

For I know the plans I have for you,"
declares the Lord,
"plans to prosper you and not to harm you,
plans to give you hope and a future."
Jeremiah 29:11

Courtney sat on the bus looking out the window at the scenery that had been the same for the past two hours and asked God to forgive her for keeping the secret from Bessie Fuller. There was no one in the community she'd just left who knew that she was expecting. Being slim and tall she was able to hide her pregnancy under full dresses and aprons. If she'd told Bessie of her condition, Bessie would never have recommended her to work for her nephew. Getting away from the community and starting afresh somewhere was an opportunity she had to grab with both hands.

Bessie had described Giles County as being in a remote area with only a few families living there, and that was very different from the two communities she'd lived in.

From Bessie's description she knew Aaron was a kind man, and from what she'd heard in his letters, the children had grown unruly, but Courtney wasn't concerned about the children. Whatever the conditions were in Giles County she'd make it work—she had to.

Her husband had died months ago when a truck ran into his buggy. They'd only been married ten months, and they hadn't known she was expecting. Besides being left penniless due to Mark's family, she also chose to leave the community in Ohio because everything reminded her of him. She'd been staying with Wilma and Peter for three months and felt that was far too long a time to be enjoying their hospitality, but they didn't seem to mind.

Whenever she was nervous or anxious about anything, her fingernails always found their way to her mouth. Once she was aware that she was biting her nails, she clasped her hands together in her lap. All her fingernails were bitten down and   looked dreadful—nail-biting was a habit she'd have to break.

The issue making her nervous right now was that she knew she'd have to confess to her new employer that she was expecting a child. With every passing moment, she grew more nervous, and she clamped her hands more tightly together, when she saw a sign beside the road: it read, 'Bells Creek,' and she knew that was the area which was her stop.

Her tummy lurched when the bus slowed.

She looked out the window and saw a lone Amish man standing tall. That must be Aaron. He looked strong and fit—well muscled with broad shoulders and dark hair poking from beneath his wide-brimmed hat. As the bus drew closer, she was surprised that he was so easy on the eyes.

"Is this your stop, Miss?" the bus driver asked as soon as he came to a halt.

Courtney rose to her feet. "Yes, it is."

The bus driver headed out of the bus to open the luggage door outside the bus as he'd done   for everyone who'd arrived at their destination that day.

She stepped out of the bus and locked eyes with Aaron. His eyes were dark brown fringed with thick dark lashes. His features were even, and she couldn't find a flaw about him. His nose was a perfect size, and his skin was tanned but not weather-beaten.

"Courtney?"

She nodded. "That's me—and you're Aaron?"

He smiled to reveal white teeth, which stood out against his dark olive skin. "I am."

Courtney reached her hand out, and he shook it.

"Just the one bag, Miss?" The driver asked.

"Yes, just the one—the brown one there." Courtney pointed to her case.

"I'll take that," Aaron said reaching down and taking the suitcase. He looked back at Courtney, and then his eyes fell to her middle. Raising his eyebrows, he asked, "Are you expecting?"

Her fingertips went straight to her mouth in shock. "I am."

Shaking his head and with no hint of his former smile, he said, "There must be some mistake. I described to Bessie the kind of nanny I was looking for and she never mentioned your condition."

"It won't stop me working."

"How can that be? This is a full-time position and in fact, it would take up most of your time. I did give my aunt a list of duties I'd need you to manage, and my three children have developed into a handful."

"I'm quite capable—*nee*— more than capable of everything you described to your aunt in your letters. She read your letters aloud to me and the list of your requirements." Since he was silent she kept going, "My husband died some months ago in an accident, and I need to get away and make a life for myself and my child."

He stepped back and tipped his hat back on his head and looked at the bus as it pulled away. Courtney knew he was wondering if he could send her back on the bus. "I don't know that you'd be able to do all the things I'd need you to do as well as look after your baby."

"I'm strong enough to do everything."

A hint of a smile touched his lips, and then he glanced down at her bag. Looking up at her face he asked, "When is your baby due?"

"Eight weeks. Please give me a chance; you won't be disappointed. Just give me a chance?"

"Since you're already here I suppose we'll both have to make the best of things until I can work something else out."

This was not the response that Courtney wanted. Now she felt as though everything was up in the air. "I thought this was to be a permanent position."

"So did I," he said nodding toward his waiting buggy. "There's my buggy."

Chapter 5

For in this hope we were saved.
Now hope that is seen is not hope.
For who hopes for what he sees?
But if we hope for what we do not see,
we wait for it with patience.
Romans 8: 24-25

Aaron was furious that his aunt would send a woman in Courtney's condition to be his nanny. He'd write to Aunt Bessie as soon as he got home and express his disappointment in her choice. The last thing he needed was someone else to look after and be responsible for. Bessie was supposed to send him someone to look after his children— cook and clean— that's all he wanted. Well, that and tend the animals. Surely there would be many women she could have chosen over a woman who was to deliver a child in eight weeks.

Even if Courtney could handle the work as she claimed, an attractive woman like she wouldn't stay for too long before she found a husband. Aaron had wanted an older woman who would be focused on his children and household. He glanced over his shoulder at Courtney as she followed him to his buggy. He couldn't be rude to her no matter how upset he was. It wasn't her fault that his aunt had made a dreadful error in judgment.

"The buggy's this way," he grunted as he looked back at her.

"I can see it," she said trying to catch up to him.

Realizing he wasn't being polite, he stopped and waited for her to draw closer. "I'm sorry, the last thing I want is to be rude. I'm in shock—that's all. You're not what I expected." *Or anything like what I'd asked for.*

"I can understand that. I'm just here to do a good job for you. That's all I want to do."

"My aunt didn't tell me of your condition."

"She might not have known."

He raised his eyebrows. "Hard to miss, though, don't you think?"

She remained silent. No one else had guessed—

her large dresses and aprons had done a good job of keeping her increasing size hidden. As they had reached the buggy, she stopped still and stared at him, but her lips didn't move.

Turning his head from her, he placed her bag in the back of the buggy. "Need a hand up?"

"Nee, I'm able to do it myself." And seeming to drive another point home to him, she added, "I'm able to do everything myself."

He sharply nodded his head. *"Gut!"*

She climbed into the buggy the same moment as he did.

"Do you live far from here?" she asked.

"Not far, only fifteen minutes away."

"It looks like a pretty place."

"It can be tough out here." As he slapped the reins against the horse for him to move forward, he glanced over to see her smiling. "I don't know if my aunt told you or not, but you'll be in a separate cabin, of course."

"Jah, she told me that, and she told me as much as she could about you and your *kinner.* She said

she hasn't been out here herself, but she read to me from some of your letters where you described it."

What else was in those letters? He'd often used his aunt as a sounding board and a confidant. Surely she wouldn't have revealed his personal words of heartache to a stranger.

"And where are you from? My aunt said you haven't been in Lancaster County for very long."

"I moved away from Ohio after my husband died. There was nothing left there for me. I have no family of my own. My husband's *familye* is still living in Ohio."

"Surely his *familye* became your *familye* once you married." He glanced over to see her frown. There was more to her story than she was letting on—he sensed some secret hurt. What else would motivate an attractive woman like her to come to an isolated place to look after someone else's children?

"It's complicated."

"Things often are," he said as he turned his attention back to the dirt-packed road the horse was clip-clopping down.

"Tell me about your *kinner*. Your aunt told me a little about them. I'm so looking forward to meeting them."

He smiled. "The oldest is Jared and he's eight. Ben is six, and Amy has just turned four. I've not seen any children with more energy than my three. I'm afraid they've tired out my poor *schweschder*-in-law, Heather. She's been looking after them, as well as her three boys."

"And are your *schweschder*-in-law's *kinner* around the same ages?"

"They are."

"That would be a handful for her."

Aaron couldn't help but chuckle. "Jared is a prankster and is always ready for a laugh and a joke. Poor old Ben is often the one who has the jokes played on him, but he's so placid he doesn't mind. Then there's Amy, and with no young girls around, I have a hard time getting her to see that she must wear a dress. I've got no idea what I'm going to do when the time comes when she must wear a prayer *kapp.*" He shook his head.

Courtney giggled. "Sounds like I came just in time."

He studied her. "I hope so. I did want someone who'd see this as something of a long-term situation and not just something to idly pass the time."

"I'm well aware of that. Your aunt told me your situation exactly. We had many long discussions about you and your *familye.*"

"You did?"

She nodded.

He shook his head. "How do you expect to fulfill your duties once your *boppli* arrives?"

"Women have been working hard, birthing babies, and continuing to work for thousands of years. I'm strong, and more than capable of doing anything I have to do."

"You are confident that you can look after your *boppli* and look after my three *kinner?*"

"I can. I know I can."

"Don't forget, you haven't met them yet. Have you looked after children before?"

"Jah! I come from a community where there were loads of them, and I grew up with a household full of them. I'm an only child myself, but I was taken in by a *familye* when I was three and raised with many children. When I got older, I started to look after many of the younger ones. If Bessie had any doubts about me, she wouldn't have recommended me, and she told me you said you would be happy with her choice."

She had him there. He did write those exact words in one of his letters to his aunt. Courtney seemed keen and had a ready answer to his questions so maybe she might work out.

She wriggled uncomfortably. "If I don't do a *gut* job for you, you can send me back."

"We shall see. Our first stop will be my *bruder's haus* to collect my *kinner.* My *schweschder*-in-law has been looking after them today. In the mornings, I've been taking them there, and collecting them at night."

"I can see that wouldn't be an ideal situation."

She turned to face him. "What's your

schweschder-in-law's name?"

"Heather and my *bruder* is James. And here we are right now."

Chapter 6

Put on then, as God's chosen ones,
holy and beloved, compassionate hearts,
kindness, humility, meekness, and patience,
bearing with one another and,
if one has a complaint against another, forgiving each
other; as the Lord has forgiven you, so you also must
forgive.
Colossians 3:12-13

Aaron had made no secret about his disappointment in her. He hadn't expected a woman with a child on the way, and Courtney had known that would've been the case. She'd hidden her pregnancy from everyone in the community with her big dresses, but Aaron had guessed right away. Possibly the people who saw her regularly didn't take too much notice of her appearance but someone seeing her for the first time would've wondered. It was only fair of him to ask her right away if she were pregnant—normally an Amish man wouldn't have inquired that of a woman, but as her employer he had a right to know.

Nervousness gnawed at her stomach as she stepped down from the buggy. Courtney was always apprehensive about meeting others for the first time. She knew she'd get along with the children just fine, but she didn't always get along with adults. One thing she had to find out about was a midwife, and Courtney couldn't leave it too long to inquire where the nearest one was. Today was possibly not the best time to mention her pregnancy or to ask any questions—it was clear it was already a sore topic with Aaron.

After they'd met the bishop and his wife who were extremely friendly and younger than she'd expected, Aaron made their excuses saying they had to collect the children.

Once back in the buggy he said, "My *haus* is only another five minutes away from my *bruder's.*"

"Do you want me to come in with you?" She figured it was enough for one day just meeting the bishop and his wife.

"Jah, of course, you have to meet Heather and James."

Courtney swallowed her nervousness and took a step forward. What if they didn't like her? There would be nothing better than for Heather to become a good friend. She hadn't had one of those for a long time.

Without knocking, Aaron walked through the door leaving Courtney unsure of whether she should follow behind him or wait to be asked inside.

As soon as he was inside, Aaron turned to face her. "Come along."

She took a step into the house. After a quick look around the darkness inside, she heard laughter coming from the kitchen. Then like a tornado, three children squealed and barreled toward Aaron. Close behind them were three boys, whom Courtney guessed to be their cousins—Heather and James' boys.

"What have I told you about running in the *haus?"* Aaron asked them in an angry tone.

"And screaming," added a woman who stepped into the room. When the woman looked up at Courtney, she smiled. "Courtney, it's so nice to meet you."

"Denke. You're Heather?"

"*Jah,* I should've said that," the woman said with a grin.

Courtney studied the small happy woman, and she liked her right away. She had pale skin with a smattering of freckles over her nose and cheeks. As soon as Heather had given Courtney a big smile, Courtney knew they'd become friends.

"Now all of you listen to me. This is Miss Courtney, and you must do everything she tells you." Heather wagged her finger at the children who were now staring at Courtney with mischievous grins on their faces.

Aaron placed his hand on top of each child's head as he named them in turn.

"I'm very pleased to meet all of you. And are these your cousins?" She looked over at the boys who were standing next to their mother.

Jared, the oldest boy said, "They're the cousins, Kyle, Garth, and Redman."

"Hello." Courtney nodded to them.

After the cousins said hello back, Heather stepped toward her. "Come and have some tea or something to eat. You must be exhausted from your long trip."

Courtney looked at Aaron who shook his head, and said, "We must go *denke,* Heather. If we get home before dark, I can show Courtney around the place."

"Jah, of course. They've just finished their hot chocolates, so they're ready to go. They've been excitedly waiting for you, Courtney."

"That's *gut.* I've been waiting to meet all of you too," Courtney said to the children.

"Come on everyone," Aaron yelled in a loud voice that made Courtney jump.

"We're so glad that you've come Courtney," Heather said. "I'll come and visit you soon. The *schul* is just up there on the hill, so when you take the children there tomorrow, you can come   here and visit me."

"*Denke,* and please come and visit whenever you find the time."

The three children ran past Courtney and got into the buggy before Courtney or Aaron had a chance to get outside.

"Don't run," Aaron said. He turned to Courtney and shook his head. "As I said, they're very lively."

"I can see that, but that's good because it shows they're bright and healthy."

Aaron raised his eyebrows and laughed. He turned and thanked Heather for looking after the children.

Just before Courtney walked out the door, Heather said, "I'm really glad you're here."

"*Denke.* I'm glad to be here too. I need a fresh start, and I think it'll be a good fit for me."

Heather leaned in and whispered, "Don't mind Aaron, he can be gruff sometimes, but he's really a pussycat deep down."

"Is he?" Courtney hoped that was true.

"You'll find that out."

Just as Aaron was nearly at the buggy, he turned back. "Come on, Miss Courtney."

"Come on, Miss Courtney," one of the children echoed.

"I'm coming," Courtney called, and then she turned back to Heather. "I'll see you soon?"

"I'll see you soon, Courtney."

She headed to the buggy and laughed as she saw three heads stuck out of the buggy staring at her. After climbing into the front seat with Aaron, she turned around to talk to the children. "Jared, Ben, and Amy, is that right?"

The two younger children giggled, and Jared said, "His name is Silly-Billy, and her name is Froggy."

"Silly-Billy and Froggy? I'll have to remember that. Are those your nicknames or your real names?" She asked the question as seriously as she could.

The three of them giggled while their father turned the buggy around.

"Quiet down. Miss Courtney isn't used to noisy

children. Now Jared, remind Miss Courtney the real names of your *bruder* and *schweschder.*"

"Ben and Amy," Jared answered in a small voice.

Ben poked an elbow in Jared's side, and then Jared poked him back. The three children giggled as they continued to poke one another.

Aaron glanced behind him, shook his head, and then turned to Courtney. "I hope you'll be happy with your cabin. I've made it as comfortable as I could. It's only small so it won't take long for the fire to warm it in the cold weather. Everything's there for you so you'll never have to come to the main house once the children are in bed, and you're finished for the day."

"*Denke*, I'm sure I'll be comfortable with whatever you've arranged for me."

Courtney had found the children to be delightful, but Aaron seemed to be irritated by her. That had to be due to the fact that she was pregnant and hadn't told anyone. She would've told him and Bessie if she'd thought it was going to hinder her ability to be a good nanny. She'd have to have at least one day off when she was giving birth, but in his letters to Bessie, Aaron had mentioned that she'd have one day a week to herself. How hard could it be to have a baby and then look after a household and small children? She'd teach the children to help with the chores as soon as she could, that is, if Aaron hadn't already taught them.

"Here we are," Aaron said pointing up a long gravel road to a cottage with a small building peeking out from the rear of it. "That's our home and next to it is your cabin, but you can't see it too well until you're nearly there because it's behind the *haus*. The *haus* looks rough from the outside, and it needs some work, but your place is all new."

Chapter 7

But the fruit of the Spirit is love, joy,
peace, patience, kindness, goodness,
faithfulness, gentleness, self-control;
against such things there is no law.
Galatians 5:22-23

Courtney looked out at Aaron's house. It was nothing grand and nothing near as big as the homes she'd been used to in Lancaster County or in Ohio. When they drew closer, she saw that the main house was little more than a cabin itself. The porch was enclosed so there was nowhere to sit outside and enjoy the beginning or the end of the day, as she liked to do. The front door was placed right in the center of the house with the built-in-porch on one side and a large window on the other.

The home was painted an attractive red color with white window frames. The lower level of the home looked like it had been added on to at one point. The upper level looked only big enough   to be used as a bedroom as it didn't cover the entire length of the house. The roof was a dark color and from where she was, it was impossible to see what it was made from, but whatever it was there were pieces lifting up. There was no doubt that the roof would soon be in need of repair—if it wasn't already.

She had to make a good impression on Aaron and have him allow her to stay on. He stopped the horse outside the house.

"If you get the children inside, Jared can show you around. After that, I can take you to see your cabin when I'm through with rubbing the horse down."

"Okay." Courtney climbed down from the buggy and attempted to help the children down. The two boys avoided her attempts to help them and jumped down by themselves. Amy had her arms outstretched, and Courtney picked her up—immediately Amy flung her small chubby arms around Courtney's neck. Once they were two steps away from the buggy, Courtney attempted to place

Amy on the ground, but Amy hung on.

"Carry me," Amy insisted.

"I'll take you two more steps, but then you must walk on your own. You're a big girl now—only *bopplis* get carried."

"I *am* a *boppli*," Amy whined.

Courtney laughed. "You're a big girl. Now come on, I'll hold your hand while your *bruder* shows me your lovely *haus*."

"Okay."

After being placed on the ground, Amy grabbed Courtney's hand and smiled up at her. Courtney had felt an immediate bond with all the children and knew they'd get along wonderfully. With Amy keeping a tight grip on her hand, she walked through the front door. The place was neat and tidy—that was her first impression.

"I'll show you the bedrooms," Jared said, as he turned and walked away with his brother close beside him.

"Denke," Courtney replied.

"This is my bedroom," Jared said showing her to

the enclosed porch.

"It's lovely and very tidy. And you even made the bed."

Ben giggled. *"Dat* tells us we have to make the bed."

"Jah, or we get into trouble," Amy added.

"Now I'll show you Ben's bedroom." Jared hurried away with Ben laughing and following after him poking him in the back. Pushing the door open with a huge grin on his face, Jared said, "And here it is."

"Another lovely tidy room," Courtney said to Ben. "Now where's Amy's room?"

Ben opened a door across the hall from his room.

"Dat said I was showing her," Jared said lunging forward and slapping his brother.

Courtney wasn't certain what to do. She'd only just arrived, and Jared had been so pleased to show her around; on the other hand, she had to tell him that he shouldn't hit his brother.

"I think Ben was just excited, and maybe he thought I was asking him where Amy's room was."

"Nee, he didn't. He heard *Dat* say that I should show you the *haus."*

"He's a little younger than you and sometimes we have to forgive the younger ones for their enthusiasm, don't you think, Jared?"

Jared shrugged his shoulders while glared at Ben. Courtney noticed Ben was smirking at Jared.

"Anyway, let's have a look at Amy's room." She stuck her head into the room. This was the smallest of all the rooms, with room for a bed and a dresser, and little else. "Did you make your bed too, Amy?"

Amy nodded.

"We have to help her," Jared said.

"That's lovely. Brothers and sisters should always help each other."

"Do you want to see *Dat's* room?" Jared asked.

"Is that the one upstairs?"

Jared nodded.

"Nee, I don't think I need to see that one. What about the kitchen?"

"This way," Jared said, and then had to run to get in front of Ben, who was racing off toward the kitchen.

Holding Amy's hand, Courtney stepped into the kitchen to see that it was the largest room in the house. There was a large dining table with eight chairs, an open fireplace with a wood-burning stove, and behind the fireplace was a stacked-rock feature wall. "It's lovely in here."

"The bathroom is through that door at the back of the *haus,*" Jared said pointing to the end of the kitchen opposite the stove.

"Gut." She looked down at the table in front of her. "There is plenty of room for us to sit around this table," Courtney said leaning with both hands on the table. "Where is the food kept, Jared?"

"In here." Jared opened a door next, to reveal a huge utility room with a cold box in the corner.

"Here you are. Has Jared finished showing you around?"

"Jah, and he's done a good job. I've seen where the children sleep, and I know where everything is. Shall I start on dinner now? It'll be dark soon."

"We've all cooked you dinner. We did it

yesterday; it just needs reheating."

"Really?" She looked at the three children who nodded, looking pleased with themselves. "That's so nice of you, *denke.*"

Amy giggled. "I helped too."

"That's *wunderbaar. Denke* everyone. I'm looking forward to tasting it."

"Dat did most of it," Ben said.

"I've put your bags at the cabin door. I'll just get the keys and take you to it."

"Can we come?" Jared asked.

"Nee, the three of you can stay here and set the table ready for dinner. Jared, you're in charge. We won't be long."

"Okay, *Dat.*"

Courtney walked out of the house with Aaron close behind.

"Our *haus* is only small, but it suits us. It needs a few odd jobs done here and there, which I will get to before the cold weather comes."

"It's a lovely home, and I think it would be cozy

when it turns cold."

"It gets the warmth from the fire and the wood stove. I'm afraid your cabin only has a small stove, but it does have the fireplace. You'll be eating with us most of the time anyway." They turned the corner of the house, and Courtney got a good look at the cabin. It was small and dove gray with white painted window frames.

"It's lovely. It looks so new and fresh." There was a small porch, double front doors, and an area where she could plant a garden.

"It's all new, and there should be everything here that you need. Heather made sure you had towels and sheets and all those bits and pieces that women think of. Anyway, I'll show you." He stepped up onto the porch and pushed the key into the lock.

Courtney was pleased that he seemed to have forgotten about her keeping her pregnancy from him. He pushed the door open, and she stepped through to see a small couch facing the fireplace, and a low coffee table between the two. "This will suit me just fine."

"You haven't seen all of it yet." He pointed to a closed door. "That's your bedroom."

She stepped forward and opened the door. There was a single bed, a dresser and a row of clothes pegs. The floorboards in the bedroom were polished the same as the living room.

"As I said, Heather made sure you'd have the correct sheets, pillowcases and all those things."

"That was nice of her. I'll have to be sure to thank her."

"I'll bring your suitcase in, as soon as I show you through."

"Denke."

He pointed to another door. "That's your bathroom and the only one in the *haus.*"

"I'll only need one."

"Now it's just the kitchen, and that'll be it. It's only big enough for you to do a small amount of cooking or boil a pot of water."

The kitchen was off from the living room, and close to the stove was a small area with a stool where she could sit by a small countertop overhang for a snack or a hot drink.

"It's so new and lovely."

"I hope you'll be happy here."

"*Jah,* I will. I'm certain I will." He frowned and looked at the ground. Courtney thought he was going to raise the subject of her pregnancy, so she quickly added, "I'll freshen up and come back to the haus to help with serving the dinner."

"I think you can have a rest tonight. The dinner only needs reheating, and the children can set the table and clean up afterward. You can start work tomorrow. How does that sound?"

"That sounds *gut, denke.*"

He strode toward the door and pulled her suitcase through the door. "Where would you like it?"

"Just there is fine."

"Okay. I'll see you in around an hour for dinner?"

"That would be perfect."

"In the kitchen, I've left a notebook where I've written down our routine. Where we buy food from, what time we leave home to go to the meetings, and *schul*—that kind of thing."

"*Denke,* I'll read it tonight."

When he'd gone, she carried the suitcase to her room and placed it on her bed. After she clicked it open, she slumped onto the bed and wondered whether she'd done the right thing in coming here. The children were adorable, but maybe someone else might have been a better choice for the young family. Even though she was convinced she could do it all, what if she couldn't? What if she fell ill? Who would look after her? *I won't get sick—I can't. I have to remain well and healthy.*

This was the place where she would stay and make a life for herself. Aaron had already accepted her—although reluctantly. She would make friends and raise her baby in the small community of Giles County.

Chapter 8

The Lord is slow to anger and great in power,
and the Lord will by no means clear the guilty.
His way is in whirlwind and storm,
and the clouds are the dust of his feet.
Nahum 1:3

After Courtney had brushed off the small pangs of doubt about coming to Giles County, she unpacked her clothing, and then took a better look around the cabin.

Tomorrow she would write to Bessie, Wilma and Peter, to let them know that she'd arrived safely.

When she walked to the house just before dinnertime, she saw three small heads looking out the window of the main house. When she stepped up to the front door, it swung open and she saw Jared's smiling face.

"*Denke,* Jared," she said as she stepped inside. Amy immediately held her hand and smiled up at her while Ben stayed close by Jared. Aaron appeared at the end of the room wiping his hands on a towel.

"Ah, there you are. Are you ready for the meal?"

"I certainly am."

"Come through; it's ready. I just have to serve it up."

Courtney sat down at the table with the children.

"I feel strange sitting here while you serve the food, Aaron. Are you sure I can't help?"

"*Nee*, you can do it from tomorrow forward. Tonight you are our guest."

"Well, I will make the most of that." She looked at the children. "And who set the table?"

"All of us did," Jared said, "except *Dat*."

"You've done a wonderful job. I couldn't have done better myself."

After Aaron placed all the dishes in the middle of the table, he sat down. They all closed their eyes and said their silent prayer of thanks for the food.

Aaron stood up and dished the food onto the children's plates. "Do you want me to serve you too?" he asked Courtney.

Courtney smiled and handed him her plate. *"Jah."*

When they had food in front of each of them Aaron said to the children, "You can start now."

"These vegetables look lovely. Do you grow these yourself?"

"We used to grow all of our own food, but lately we haven't had time. I'm afraid our poor old vegetable patch has become strangled with weeds. These are from the market gardens."

"We could start growing a vegetable garden again." She looked at the children. "Would you like that?"

They nodded, and Amy said, "I want to grow things."

"Me too," Ben said.

"Me too." Jared laughed.

Courtney loved to be around children with such innocent and positive energy. "Then that's what we shall do. I'm fairly certain at this time of year we can plant greens like cabbage, cauliflower and kale. I haven't had a good look around the property.

Where does it start and end?"

After Aaron had told her, Courtney asked where the best place would be to start their vegetable garden.

"Near the fruit trees. I'll have the children show you where the peach trees are tomorrow.

"We'll soon have lots of peaches to eat. There are a lot on the trees," Jared said.

"There aren't a lot." Ben laughed.

"There are so." Jared scowled at Ben.

"Now no arguing at the table. You must be on your good behavior for Miss Courtney."

"Jah, Dat," Jared said.

"For dessert we have the children's favorite and they thought you might like it too."

"What is it?"

"It's cheesecake with strawberries, cream and ice-cream."

"Oh, I love that."

While Aaron served the dessert, he explained who was who in their small community.

After dinner, Courtney insisted on helping wash

up. "I'd love to wash up and the children can help me. Would you like that?" she asked the children who all nodded.

"I'll help," Amy replied.

"Me too," Ben said.

"I'll do it too," Jared said.

"Okay if all of you are happy to do it, I'll sit out in the living room and make that fire nice and warm.

"Would you like a cup of hot tea or a cup of *kaffe?*" Courtney asked Aaron.

His face brightened. "I would love a *kaffe.* Jared will show you where everything is."

Although Courtney knew that Aaron wasn't altogether happy with her presence, he must've had some kind of relief that he didn't have to look after the children and do his work every day. Now there was someone to cook and care for his children. Once she'd organized the children with the washing up, she put the pot on to boil for a cup of coffee. Once she had it made she took it out to him and placed it on the table beside him.

He looked up at her and smiled. *"Denke.* How are they doing with the cleaning up?"

"Very well."

"Why don't you sit down with me and rest awhile?"

She sat down. "I've been doing nothing but sit the whole day."

"Jah, but sitting on a bus is tiring."

"I guess that's true."

"I am sorry I reacted the way that I did when I saw you. It wouldn't have made you feel welcome."

She tugged at the strings of her prayer *kapp.* "I wouldn't have come if I didn't think I could do a good job. I'm not taking advantage of you and neither will I—ever. I believe in doing an honest day's work and that's what I'll be doing for you."

He studied her for a moment. "I believe it, and apparently so does Bessie although she didn't know of your condition."

Courtney looked down at the ground. "I'm sorry about that; I just didn't think it was relevant."

He pursed his lips. "I think it would be most

relevant, but what's done is done. I already feel a burden lifted from my shoulders having you here and if *Gott* wills it things will stay that way." He took a sip of coffee.

His calm nature and personality had a soothing effect on Courtney's nerves. She settled into the couch a little more.

"I'm sorry, you don't have any *kaffe*. I'll get you some."

"Nee denke. I'm not much of a *kaffe* drinker especially right after dinner." As her pregnancy had advanced Courtney found she had to eat smaller amounts of food, and eat more often, rather than having large meals. The baby seemed to be taking up all the room leaving her stomach little room for food.

"We've finished. Come and see," Jared said as he approached the couch.

"Jared, you must say 'excuse me' when adults are talking."

"Sorry, *Dat.* Excuse me."

"Jah, Jared?" Aaron asked.

"Please come and see the kitchen, Miss Courtney?"

Courtney stood. "I'd love to have a look at it."

"I'll come and see too," Aaron said standing up.

Jared's face flushed with a huge smile as he led them both to the kitchen. When they entered the kitchen, Ben and Amy were standing, smiling and waiting to see what the adults would say.

"Well, that's *wunderbaar.* I couldn't have done a better job myself," Courtney said.

"Jah, you've done a *gut* job. All of you," Aaron agreed.

"I did the most," Ben said.

Jared clamped his hands on his hips. *"Nee,* you didn't."

"I did," said Amy with a giggle that made her brothers giggle too.

"You've all done good work," Courtney said.

"Jah, you have." Aaron turned to Courtney. "After dinner, I usually tell them stories."

Courtney nodded, wondering whether she should go or stay.

Aaron added, "You're welcome to stay and listen if you'd like."

"*Jah*, stay please," Amy said taking hold of her hand.

"I would love to as long as no one minds."

"We want you to stay," Jared said, and then Ben echoed his words.

"Then I shall stay."

The three children ran out to the living room.

"We generally sit in front of the fire while I tell them Bible stories and then they go to bed."

"Okay," Courtney said while following Aaron to the couch.

The three children were on the couch and they moved over when Courtney approached, to make room for her. When Courtney sat, Amy scooted onto her lap.

"Amy, don't sit on Miss Courtney's lap."

Courtney moved her forward a little. "It's okay with me if she sits like this, if you don't mind."

"All right." Aaron sat down on the lounge chair next to the couch.

"Tell us about the three men in the fire, *Dat,*" Ben said, leaning forward toward his father.

"*Jah,* that one," Jared said with his face beaming.

Aaron chuckled and explained to Courtney, "That's their favorite."

"It's a favorite of mine too."

Chapter 9

The Lord is slow to anger and abounding in
steadfast love,
forgiving iniquity and transgression,
but he will by no means clear the guilty,
visiting the iniquity of the fathers on the children,
to the third and the fourth generation
Numbers 14:18

Aaron began the children's favorite bedtime story.

"Hundreds of years ago there was a king who made a rule that everyone in the land had to bow down to a great golden statue that he had made. They were to bow down before it whenever the king ordered special music to be played. Everyone in the land was so frightened of the king that they all bowed down and worshipped the statue. Everyone that is, except three men named Shadrach, Meshach, and Abednego. Before long, word got back to the king that these three men had

75

refused to obey his rules. He called for the men to be brought before him. King Nebuchadnezzar asked Shadrach, Meshach, and Abednego whether it was true that they disobeyed him. They said that it was true, and then the king, feeling a little kindly toward the men offered to give them one more chance. If the music played again and they bowed down and worshipped, then they'd be free to go. If they didn't, what did the king tell them would happen?"

"They'd be thrown into the fire," Ben said.

"That's right."

"Keep going," Jared urged his father.

"He said that their God would not be able to save them. The three men saw the burning fire and knew the king would throw them in if they didn't bow down next time. But they remembered the word of God that says that you should not worship any other gods. Now they could've thought that it wouldn't hurt to pretend to worship the golden statue, but they feared the judgement of God more than the king and his fire. They knew they had to obey God rather than men. They told the king that God would save them from the fire and they would never serve his gods or worship any images made by the hand of man. The king became furious and ordered that the fire be heated seven times hotter than it had ever been heated before."

"Nee," Amy said, wrapping her hands around her knees, her eyes wide open.

"Then the king ordered the men to be tied up. The fire was so hot that no one could get near it. The king's men couldn't even get close enough to it to throw the three men into it. But the king didn't care. He ordered his strongest men to throw Shadrach, Meshach, and Abednego into the fire. The men who threw them in fell to the ground and died because they were overcome with the heat of the flames. The king didn't care. He was glad to be rid of the three men who'd disobeyed him, and he was sure they were dead.

But then someone noticed there was someone standing in the fire and he yelled out to alert the king. The king didn't believe it but he looked in the fiery furnace and didn't see one man. How many did he see?"

"Four men," the three children yelled out.

"*Jah*, there were four men in the fire. The king was astonished, as he'd only had three thrown in the fire and all three of them should be dead, but there surely shouldn't have been four living men. Word traveled that people said the fourth man looked like a son of the gods. The king hurried from his throne and cried to the three men and ordered them out. He said to them, 'Servants of the Most High God, come out!' They came out, and their clothes weren't even burned."

Courtney saw Ben and Jared's eyes wide like saucers. She would've loved someone telling her stories when she was a child, but she had no one giving her devoted attention like Aaron was giving his children.

"And you know what else?"

"Their clothes didn't smell like smoke," Amy said.

"And the fire had only burned the ropes around

them," added Jared.

"That's right and that's our *Gott*. We serve a powerful *Gott* who is able to do wondrous things and we need to follow him and do what he says and he will watch over us and keep us safe."

It gladdened Courtney's heart to see the look of wonder on the young faces. She looked across at Aaron and they exchanged smiles.

"Well, it's off to bed with you now," Aaron said.

"One more story?" Ben asked with a pout.

"Not tonight. You've got a big day ahead of you tomorrow."

"What are we doing tomorrow?" Jared asked.

"You all have to show Miss Courtney around and tell her where everything is. And you have to help her all you can."

"We will," Amy said in a tiny voice before she opened her mouth widely and yawned.

"Will you tuck us in, Miss Courtney?" Ben asked.

Courtney looked at Aaron who said, "We can both tuck you in and you each have to get used to sleeping in your own rooms. Jared you take Ben and Amy and all of you wash up and clean your teeth, and we'll be along soon."

The three children headed to the bathroom.

"They are very well-behaved."

He scoffed. "Only because I keep at them. They aren't as well-behaved as I'd like them to be, but at the same time I don't believe in cruelty to keep them in line."

"Nee, neither do I. All children need understanding and kindness."

"That's what Bessie said you believed."

"Oh, I didn't tell her that."

"You didn't?"

Courtney shook her head.

"She must have guessed." He smiled.

"Maybe," she said back, frowning a little.

The children passed them and went to their rooms.

"This is good. I can see how you put them in bed so I'll know what to do when you're not here."

"I hope I'll be here all the time." He stared at her

as he rose from the couch. "But there might be the odd occasion you'll need to put them to bed."

She stood. "I'll follow you."

He walked towards Jared's room first and said over his shoulder. "I always start with the oldest first. The oldest always has privileges. He gets to ride in the front of the buggy when there's no other adult traveling with me."

"Okay. I'll remember that."

He kneeled down beside Jared's bed and pulled the quilt up around his neck. "Sleep tight, Jared. Say your prayers." He kissed him on his forehead.

"Gut nacht, Jared."

"Gut nacht, Dat; gut nacht, Miss Courtney."

They walked out of the room and Aaron closed the door behind him. Courtney walked to the other two bedrooms and waited by the door for Aaron to walk through. He walked into Ben's room and followed the same routine except, after his father kissed him on the forhead, Ben raised his arms to Courtney.

Courtney glanced at Aaron and after a nod

from him, she leaned down and kissed Ben on his forehead. *"Gut nacht,* Ben."

"Gut nacht."

When they walked into Amy's room she was fast asleep with the top of her head poking out from under the quilt. Aaron lifted the quilt just slightly to see her sucking her thumb. Courtney smiled and Aaron looked up at her and grinned before he placed the quilt back over her.

They both crept out of the room.

"Well you must be really tired by now."

"I am a little, but I'm also excited. I'll go home and read how your home runs. I want to do everything just right."

Aaron chuckled. "I don't think there is a right or a wrong. Just do your best and we'll all be fine."

"I certainly will." She hesitated wondering if he'd want to talk to her some more.

"Shall I walk you to your cabin?"

"Nee, denke. I'll be fine. I left a lamp on. I'll soon see my way."

He nodded. "The light from the kitchen is still

on so that will light the pathway."

"*Gut nacht,* Aaron and I thank you for the job here. I will do the very best I can for you and the boys." She giggled. "Oh, and Amy."

"*Denke,* Courtney." He walked her to the door and then took her shawl off the peg and placed it around her shoulders.

Once she was out in the cold night air she hugged the shawl to herself and pushed it up around her neck. With her hair always pulled up under her *kapp,* her neck and ears were always the first to feel the cold.

She trod carefully on the silvery moonlit path until she arrived at her cabin, which was less than thirty paces from the main *haus.*

When she opened the door, a waft of warm air engulfed her. She hurried over to the fire and placed another large log into it. The cold weather wasn't here just yet, but even still, it was colder than an August night would've been back in Lancaster County.

After she changed into her nightgown, she pulled

on her warm robe and sat in front of the fire. She picked up the huge wad of papers, which held all the notes that Aaron had jotted down about how to look after his children, and their daily routines for each day of the week.

When she was nearly halfway through, she found it difficult to keep awake. Knowing that she had an early start in the morning to cook Aarons' breakfast before work, she placed the notes back on the table and went to bed.

She threw back the curtains and lay in bed watching the clouds gently roll past the stars against the backdrop of a dark blue sky. As soon as it was light she would wake. She always woke at first light and wanted to keep within that pattern.

Whenever she was nearly asleep thoughts would plague her, and tonight was no different. It pained her that her baby would grow up without knowing who his or her father was, but she couldn't let her pain pass on to her child. Nor could she allow her child to be defined by someone who'd grown up not knowing a parent. She'd seen a man in her old community who'd grown up not knowing who his father was and it played on his mind day and night—he spoke of little else. Courtney didn't want that for her child—she had to be strong. *Things will be how they will be*, is what the woman she'd called her mother had always said to her when she was growing up. *Ach, Courtney, you're such a worried girl. Things will be how they will be and no matter how much you worry you won't change anything.*

Courtney smiled as she recalled that same woman standing there with her arms folded across her chest berating her about worrying. After she exhaled heavily, she rolled over onto her side. All her movements were slower since her belly had grown larger. She was certain her belly was much more prominent in the last two days. If Bessie saw her now she would most likely guess that she was expecting.

She'd have to tell Bessie in her letter that she was expecting and she would apologize for not mentioning it right away. It was a normal thing within the community that people wouldn't discuss pregnancy, but she really should've told Bessie of her situation. Hopefully, Bessie would understand why she didn't. She put her hands over her baby and smiled. It wouldn't be long until she was face-to-face with the little person that God had blessed her with.

Chapter 10

Therefore I say unto you,
What things soever ye desire,
when ye pray, believe that ye receive them,
and ye shall have them.
Mark 11:24

While it was fresh in his mind, Aaron wanted to write to Bessie to tell her how upset he was over her sending a woman who would soon need a long time off work. Courtney seemed to be a lovely woman and she certainly had a way with children, but it just wasn't practical. He'd waited so long to find a suitable nanny that he'd had his hopes up for someone perfect—a nanny who was expecting a child herself was totally unsuited.

Dear Aunt Bessie,

I hope this letter finds you in good health. Courtney arrived safely today.

I do have to tell you that I have doubts about

her. Didn't you realize that Courtney is only a few weeks away from giving birth? I had hoped you read the part in my letters about me needing a woman to help about the place. I fear I am at risk of her adding another burden rather than removing the one I was trying to resolve.

The other thing is that Courtney is young and attractive. A woman such as she will not last long in our small town with so few women. We already have two bachelors around her age that are on the search for a wife. She will most likely get married and she'll move on. Will you please keep looking for the woman I described in my letters?

Your nephew,

Aaron

Aaron popped the letter in an envelope and sealed it. He turned off the light and made his way up to his bedroom. Once he'd turned down the gas lamp, he moved the curtain aside so he could see Courtney's cabin.

She must be asleep, he thought, as the cabin was

in darkness.

The spiraling smoke coming from the chimney, which intermingled with the moonlight in the gray starlit night, caught his attention.

Even though the woman was nothing like the one he'd envisioned, it felt comforting to have another adult close by. Maybe he shouldn't send that letter. He could write a different letter and thank Bessie for what she'd done, after all, Courtney might work out—she seemed extremely confident that she could do everything, so maybe she could. After half an hour weighing up the fors and againsts, he decided he wouldn't send the letter just yet.

What if she found a husband and left them? That was his greatest fear. A woman as attractive as Courtney would probably not be satisfied helping with raising someone else's children when she could get married again and raise her own. He took off his shirt and his trousers and threw them over the chair in the corner of the room.

It was unfair that Ellen had gone and he was left alone with their three children. He'd never   even imagined that something would happen that would tear her away from them. Small children need their mother rather than their father. Why hadn't God taken him? If he'd been given the choice he'd much rather have gone and Ellen to have stayed with the children. But, he wasn't given the choice and he must not be bitter with God for taking Ellen from them at such a young age.

He got into bed, pulled the covers up to his neck and closed his eyes tightly. A scripture came into his mind—he couldn't recall the exact words, but it was about God saying that he blessed people with old age. Why hadn't he blessed Ellen with old age? She'd been the perfect wife and mother, and she was kind and sweet. As well as that, she was devoted to living in the ways of the Lord—a good and righteous life.

Opening his eyes, he blinked back tears. God had to be testing him. Courtney arriving being just weeks away from giving birth was proof that God was testing him and giving him another trial to go through. Just when he thought that God was sending him a wonderful nanny and he could finally relax, He sent a woman who might need looking after herself.

One good thing about Courtney was that the children really liked her. He had to trust in God that the reason He sent Courtney was in his and his family's best interests. Knowing all he could do now was hope and pray, Aaron closed his eyes again and thanked God for all the good in his life. He had a roof over his head, healthy children, and he finally had a nanny who would take a lot of pressure off him—at least for the next few weeks.

* * *

Aaron woke early to the sounds of noises coming from the kitchen. He blinked a couple of times and then breathed in the smell of food cooking. It was a rare treat these days to have breakfast cooked for him.

After he took fresh clothes out of his dresser, he pulled them on, and then looked around the room wondering if Courtney might come up there to tidy up at some stage during the day. He picked up his previous day's clothes that he'd carelessly dropped onto the chair, and threw them in the clothes hamper before he headed downstairs.

"Good morning, Courtney. You're up bright and early."

Courtney swung around from the stove to face him. "Morning. I always wake up about this time. And in your notes this is what time you said you liked your breakfast." Courtney glanced up at the clock on the wall.

"That's right. I didn't know you would've had time to read it all."

Courtney gave a little giggle. "I didn't, but I did read most of it. The food's nearly cooked, are you ready for it now?"

Aaron sat down at the table. "I'm ready. You're eating with me, I hope."

As she dished the bacon and eggs onto his plate she said, *"Jah,* I thought I should eat before the children wake." She passed him the plate and then served some onto another plate for herself. Before she sat, she poured him a cup of coffee and made herself a pot of tea. When she finally sat down, she noticed he hadn't started. *"Ach,* I'm sorry, I didn't realize you were waiting for me before you gave thanks."

He smiled and then they both closed their eyes to give their silent thanks to God for the food.

She opened her eyes before he did, and for an instant she felt that time had turned back and she was sitting across from Mark. When Aaron opened his eyes, he smiled at her and she smiled back.

"This looks and smells delicious."

"I hope it tastes all right. People tell me I can cook well, but I don't cook anything fancy–just plain food."

He took a mouthful and then had some coffee. She couldn't help wondering if the food was bad and he was trying to wash the taste away. Courtney loaded some scrambled egg on her fork and placed it into her mouth hoping that their conversation over breakfast would be easy. Not knowing what to say, she kept quiet and allowed him to lead the discussion hoping he wouldn't mention her soon-to-be-born baby. She knew he didn't like the idea of her arriving as a pregnant nanny, and she didn't want the conversation to go in a negative direction so early in the day.

"Is your accommodation satisfactory?"

"*Jah,* it's *wunderbaar.* I had such a good night's sleep."

"You weren't cold?"

"*Nee,* I was as warm as toast."

"That's thanks to Heather. She helped me set it all up."

"I must thank her."

He had another mouthful of coffee. "The children won't be awake for another hour."

"That will give me time to do a few chores."

"*Nee,* don't overdo it. Take a rest where you can."

"I like to keep busy."

"You'll be kept busy enough once they're awake. When you're able to take a rest take one—that's my best advice."

Courtney smiled, wondering what she'd be in for. The children had seemed easy to handle, but she hadn't spent a full day with them.

"I'm sorry I kept my condition from you and Bessie." The words had tumbled out of her mouth before she'd thought them through.

He stared at her. "What's done is done. We'll see if this situation works out for both of us and, if either of us feels it's not working out, we should be honest and tell the other."

"That seems fair." He was giving her a fair chance to prove herself and she couldn't ask for more than that. "What are you doing today?"

"I work together with James every day. He and I share the farming land. Today we're fixing fences on the southern border. We run cattle on one side and we also grow soybeans."

"Bessie said you had a farm but never told me exactly what kind of farm."

"If you have any problems today Heather's not far from here. Do you remember how to get there?"

"I think so. Just up this road and turn left at the T intersection?"

"That's right, and use the buggy. I take the wagon. The *schul* is right next to them, and you'll need to drive the children there in the buggy and collect them after *schul*. I'll hitch it for you before I leave every morning."

"*Denke*, but you don't need to do that. I'm able to hitch the buggy." Courtney giggled. "I work for you not the other way around."

He smiled. "That's not much for me to do. I always did it for Ellen."

Courtney placed her fork down and took a sip of hot tea. "It's just that I don't want you to think that I'm not capable of doing everything any other nanny could do."

"I'll keep that in mind." He looked down at his food. "I haven't tasted food as good as this in a while."

"It's just plain scrambled egg."

"Anything that I don't have to cook tastes extra specially *wunderbaar*." He grinned which made her relax a little. "It's nice to see you smile. The only time I've seen you genuinely smile is when you've spoken to the children."

"They'd make anyone smile. I guess it's just that I'm a little nervous not knowing what you expect from me."

"I'm not an ogre. Just look after the children, cook, and do a few chores."

"I know that now, since I've read most of what you wanted. I guess I'm a little nervous about being in a new place with new people."

He nodded. "I understand." He took his last mouthful of coffee.

"More *kaffe?*"

"*Nee,* that's fine. I normally only have one in the morning and that sees me through the day." He finished off his scrambled egg and Courtney continued eating but at a much slower pace than Aaron.

"*Denke,* that was great." Aaron stood. "I'll be home today for the midday meal."

Because Courtney was still eating, she   stayed

seated. "I'll see you then."

"Enjoy your first day."

"I'm sure I will."

Chapter 11

But my God shall supply all your need
according to his riches in glory by Christ Jesus.
Philippians 4:19

Once Aaron was outside, Courtney felt a whole lot more relaxed. She tiptoed to the kitchen window to see him preparing his wagon for the day ahead. Staying well back in case he happened to glance up and see her, she studied him. There was no doubt he was an attractive man. He looked across to the window and she stepped a bit further back with her heart pumping wildly. After a while, she stood at the kitchen sink as though she were washing the dishes, but by then he had gone. Thinking it strange she didn't hear him leave, she moved into the bathroom and looked out into the fields. She saw his wagon moving away—a speck in the distance.

She moved back into the kitchen and saw Jared standing there wiping his eyes.

"Good morning, Jared."

Jared nodded, looking as though he was barely awake.

"Are you ready for breakfast?"

Jared nodded again.

"Okay you sit down and I'll make you some." Normally she would've waited for all three children to be awake before cooking, but since they would have a new routine with her there she wanted to be flexible until the children adjusted. "Do the others wake as early as you?"

"Sometimes," Jared said.

Since Ellen's death, Aaron had been getting the children up, fed, and dressed before taking them to Heather's for the workday.

"Your *vadder's* only just left. How about as soon as I make you breakfast we go out and collect the eggs?"

"That's Ben and Amy's job."

"Will they be upset if we do it?"

Jared nodded. "It used be my chore when I was little. Amy doesn't have many chores. You should give her some more."

"I certainly will; everybody should have their own special things that they do every day." Courtney noticed a smile on Jared's face at the thought of his younger sister getting more chores. She could tell Jared had a lot of mischief in him. She buttered two slices of bread and fried them in the pan. I think we might need to bake more bread today; maybe we'll leave it for this afternoon when you get home from *schul* and then we can all help."

"Boys don't cook."

"Your *vadder* cooks and has been doing so these past months. Everybody should learn to cook. It's a skill just like any other."

"*Dat* doesn't cook."

"It seems I arrived just in time." Courtney laughed and sat down for a moment to allow everything time to cook. "Your *vadder* told me he's been cooking for you for the last few months. He's written everything down for me so I know his and your routine." Now that he knew that, Jared might be less inclined to put anything over on her—she hoped.

Jared looked disappointed that she knew so much.

Courtney got up and flipped the toast over.

"Do you have a *dat?* " Jared asked unexpectedly.

Courtney picked up the wooden spoon and stirred the eggs. "I did have a *vadder* and he's gone to be with *Gott* a long time ago, the same as my *mudder*. Did you mean to ask if I have a husband?"

"*Jah*, that's what I meant."

"I had one, but he's also with *Gott.* "

Jared stared at her. "My *mudder* is with *Gott* too. A lot of people are with *Gott* now."

"*Jah,* I did hear that. I'm sure you miss her, and I miss my husband, too, but Gott is taking good care of them and one day we'll see them again." Courtney placed his eggs on a plate and then put the golden toasted bread alongside. She poured herself another cup of tea and then sat down with him.

Courtney had read in Aaron's notebook that the children's *schul* was held four days a week on

Heather and James' land. There were only twelve children in the school ranging in ages from five through ten. That had to mean that, with Aaron's oldest two and James and Heather's three, they made up nearly half the students. "Do you like your schoolwork, Jared?"

Jared was busily eating his eggs, but he put his fork down and said, "Sometimes."

She had been hoping for more of a conversation. "And your sister Amy is too young to go yet, isn't she?"

"Jah, too little."

"What do you like learning about at school?"

"Nothing. I don't want to go to *schul* but   *Dat* says we must."

Courtney laughed. "There must be something you like learning about."

"It's just words and numbers. Sometimes we play games."

"Really? What kind of games?"

"Games about words and numbers."

The other two children interrupted Jared and

Courtney.

"Everyone's awake now. *Gut* morning you two. Would you like breakfast?"

Ben nodded while Amy remained silent and ran to the bathroom. Courtney put more toast on and got more eggs ready. Soon Amy reappeared. "Have you washed your hands?" Courtney asked Amy.

Amy nodded and sat down in between Jared and Ben. It seemed none of them were very active in the morning. After breakfast they all did their chores, and then they got ready for *schul.*

Courtney drove the boys to *schul* with Jared sitting in the front giving her directions. When the boys were safely inside the one room schoolhouse, she and Amy headed back home. She didn't feel she knew Heather well enough to drop by her house even though she'd been invited to do so.

"Are you looking forward to going to *schul* when you're bigger, Amy?"

"*Jah,* I want to go with the boys."

Courtney remembered what Aaron said about Amy not wanting to wear a dress because her brothers didn't. "You'll be going to *schul* soon enough and you can play with some other girls there."

When Courtney had unhitched the buggy, Amy took hold of her hand and together they walked inside. "Looks like our fire's gone out. Are you cold?"

Amy shook her head.

"Perhaps we'll leave it for a while and light it when we get home after collecting the boys."

"Okay."

"Are you hungry?"

When Amy shook her head, Courtney tried to remember what was on her list of chores. She knew she had to bake bread every couple of days and she knew from cooking breakfast that the bread supply was running low. "How would you like to help me make bread?"

"*Jah.* Can I do it?"

"I did say the boys could help me, but Jared wasn't too keen on that idea, so maybe you and I will do it by ourselves." Just at that moment, they heard the sound of a horse and buggy.

Amy raced to the window to see who it was and Courtney wasn't far behind her.

"It's Aunty Heather."

"*Wunderbaar.* Let's go and greet her."

Amy grabbed Courtney's hand, pulled the door open, and tugged her outside.

They both waited until Heather climbed out of the buggy.

"Hello," Courtney said and then Amy said hello.

"Hello to you both." Heather hurried toward them. "Did you find the *schul* all right?"

"*Jah,* I had two helpers to show me the way."

"*Jah,* of course you would've."

"Come in. I'm so pleased you've come for a visit. Will you stay for a cup of tea or *kaffe?*"

"I've just taken the boys to *schul* so I've got some free time."

When they were sitting at the table with hot tea, Courtney said, "I need to do some baking. I can offer you sugar cookies and that's all."

"They're fine sugar cookies. I should know I

baked them."

Courtney giggled. "It must've been a lot of extra work for you helping Aaron out with the children." Courtney looked over at Amy who was sitting at the table with a hot chocolate.

"In times of trouble we all work together. He'd do the same if the situation called for it."

"I'm sure he would. I'm so glad you stopped by today because I have something to ask you."

"What is it?"

"Do you know a midwife? Is there one around here somewhere?" Courtney bit her lip hoping that there was, otherwise she wasn't quite sure what she was going to do.

Heather looked over at Amy and then leaned in to whisper, "Are you having a *boppli?*"

Courtney nodded.

"That's *wunderbaar.* I thought you might be, but I didn't know if I should ask in case I was wrong. I'm a midwife."

"Are you?" Courtney heaved a sigh of relief, as that was the one thing she was most concerned with.

"I'm a registered nurse with midwife training. I joined the Amish when I was twenty-two and married James. I've delivered three babies since we moved here; that's not many but there aren't a lot being born around here."

"Would you be able to deliver my *boppli?*"

"I'd be happy to. When is your due date?"

"In eight week's time."

"Have you had check ups?"

Courtney shook her head. "I moved from Ohio to Lancaster County after my husband died and when I arrived there, I was looking for a job so I didn't tell anyone about the baby and then I just kept keeping it quiet until Bessie found me the job here with Aaron."

"Come to my *haus* tomorrow after you take Ben and Jared to *schul*. I've got a blood pressure machine and the rest of my equipment there. I'll take a look at you."

"*Denke,* Heather. That's such a relief and a load off my mind."

"Are your *familye* in Ohio?"

"I have no *familye*. My husband's *familye* lived in Ohio, but he was an *Englischer* before he joined the community, and they weren't happy with him marrying me. They sold the house from underneath me because it belonged to them, and they made everything hard for me. I thought I'd have a new start in Lancaster County. I'd met nice people from the different regions there over the years. I stayed with David and Wilma Yoder for some months and they were so lovely to me."

"May I please have a cookie?" Amy asked.

"*Jah,* you can have one." Courtney passed the plate of cookies and Amy took one.

"*Denke,* Miss Courtney."

"You're welcome," Courtney said, taking a sugar cookie for herself.

"What lovely manners you have Amy," Heather said which made Amy giggle.

Courtney took a bite out of the cookie and when she'd swallowed she said, "I didn't realize that you weren't raised Amish. It didn't even occur to me."

"Most people guess from my name."

"I know it's not a traditional Amish name but that's not too unusual. Are you pleased you joined the community?"

Heather nodded. "I'm more happy than I've ever been. Mind you, I've always been a happy person, but since I met and married James he's made such a huge difference. It's a good way of life and everyone is so kind and caring just like one big happy family. A happy *familye* of *Gott* and we can always do with another *boppli* about the place. Funny that Aaron never mentioned it."

"That's the thing that makes me feel bad. Aaron didn't know because no one in Lancaster County knew, not even Bessie."

"Oh. Now it all makes sense. I thought there was something wrong with him yesterday. Is that when he found out?"

"*Jah.* Do you think he was greatly upset? He appeared to be shocked and a little disappointed that no one told him and I told him it was my entire fault. I had to convince him that I could still work and do everything right after my *boppli* is born and leading up to the birth. I might need a day off."

Heather laughed. "He didn't pack you off on the next bus. He'll get over it. He was expecting someone old and plain, I'll bet. He certainly didn't expect someone young and attractive."

Courtney smiled. She certainly hadn't felt good about herself in a long time, so it was nice to hear someone speak about her as though she were attractive. "That's nice of you to say."

Heather wagged her finger. "Now don't get prideful."

"I'm so far away from being prideful that it'll never be a concern. I just hope I didn't upset Aaron too much after everything that's happened to him. I know it's not easy to lose a spouse at such a young age, especially when it would have been so unexpected."

"That's true. He's coped well, but he has to because of his *kinner*. Life goes on—his children keep on growing and he needs to be a *vadder* to them and he can't do that if he doesn't find a way to cope with his loss. It can't have been easy for you, either." Heather drank a mouthful of tea.

Courtney shook her head. "I haven't had time to stop and feel sorry for myself. I've been too busy trying to find a way to create a life for my *boppli* and myself. I miss him dreadfully and my heart aches, but I guess just like Aaron I have to keep moving forward and put my *boppli's* needs first."

"That's true. Sorry, I must go. The chores won't get done if I stay here and talk all day. Don't forget to stop by tomorrow and I'll check you over; make sure that all looks *gut*. I'll have something for Amy to play with so she's kept busy."

"*Denke,* Heather. I'm truly grateful. And *denke* for helping Aaron fix up the cabin so nicely."

Heather nodded, stood up and walked over to Amy and kissed her on top of her head. "Bye, Amy."

"Bye bye, Aunty Heather."

"We'll come outside and wave," Courtney said standing up and putting a hand out toward Amy.

Amy slipped off her chair and put her hand in

Courtney's. Together they walked to the front door behind Heather. Heather stopped and looked down at a letter on the table by the door. "What's this?" She picked up the letter and turned it over. "It's a letter to Aaron's aunt. I can take it today since I'm going to the post office."

"That's *gut,* that will save him the time of going there himself."

Heather took the letter with her and after she drove away, Courtney looked at Amy. "What were we going to do before Aunty Heather arrived?"

Amy put her finger to her lip. "Um… bake bread."

"*Jah,* that's right. You were going to help me bake some bread."

Amy giggled.

Chapter 12

God is not a man, that he should lie;
neither the son of man, that he should repent:
hath he said, and shall he not do it?
or hath he spoken, and shall he not make it good?
Numbers 23:19

After dinner that night when the children were helping with the after-dinner cleanup, Aaron came back into the kitchen and asked about the letter to Bessie.

"Did you see it? It was by the door on the table."

"*Ach jah,* I did see it. Heather took it with her to post since she was just on her way to the post office." Courtney studied his face. "Why? Is something wrong?"

He shook his head. "*Nee.* It's okay."

"Would you like some hot tea?"

"I would, *denke.*" Aaron went back to the living room and waited by the fire for his tea. He'd decided not to send that letter wherein he'd been complaining about Courtney, and now he felt bad. She had barely been there for one whole day and already she was fitting in so well with all of them. He'd have to write another letter contradicting the one he'd sent and explain that he was surprised by her condition, but he was so grateful to Bessie for finding Courtney. He stood and walked over to his bureau to get pen and paper. While he waited, he penned a quick letter to Bessie, which he'd post the very next day.

"Here you are," Courtney said as she handed him a cup of tea.

"Wunderbaar denke." He looked up at her. "You certainly have a lovely way with children."

"I've always liked children. I wanted to have many of them and have a huge family since I didn't come from a big *familye* myself."

"I only had my *bruder,* and I always wanted a bigger *familye* when I was growing up so I know what you mean." He wanted to talk more and find out everything about her. There was something so calming about her nature.

"I'd better get back to supervising in the kitchen."
She gave a little giggle before she left.

Her laughter was like a clear ringing bell to
his ears. It had been a long time since a woman's
laughter had rung through the house like that.

* * *

Courtney pulled the buggy up right in front of
Heather's house, knowing Heather had already
taken her children to school because she'd seen the
three boys at the door of the school.

Instinctively, Courtney knew that all was right
with her baby, but still, she couldn't help thinking—
what if she was wrong? The baby was the only
reason she'd had to keep going after Mark died.

Courtney looked up and saw that Heather had
come outside and was standing between the house
and Aaron's buggy with a shawl wrapped around
her shoulders. "I think I'm running a little late this
morning. I'm sorry," Courtney said.

"That's fine; come in."

After she tied the horse's reins around the post, she walked inside with Amy hanging onto her hand.

Heather put Amy in front of some toys in the corner of the room and then she walked over and locked the front door. "That's to make sure that we won't be disturbed."

"Good idea. I'm a little nervous."

"Don't be. I'm sure everything is fine. Most births are trouble-free."

Courtney had her blood pressure taken and after she lay back on the couch, Heather pressed on the edges of her belly.

"The *boppli* is in a good position. She's unlikely to turn this late in the pregnancy."

"She?"

Heather giggled. "We need more girls around here. I'm hoping she's a girl."

"Oh. Does it happen, though? Does the *boppli* ever turn this late?"

"*Jah,* but you'll know if it happens—it'll be uncomfortable. There we go; all done." She reached out and helped Courtney to a sitting position.

"That's it?"

"That's all we need at this stage. All looks good so there's no reason to take your blood for testing as long as you've been healthy. Have your ankles been swelling?"

"*Nee* and I've been on my feet most days."

"And you haven't been feeling dizzy or anything?"

Courtney shook her head.

"Those are all good signs that say both you and the baby are healthy."

Courtney heaved a sigh of relief. "*Denke* so much. I'm so glad you're a midwife. That solves so many problems and takes a load off my shoulders like you wouldn't believe."

Heather gave a little giggle. "Let's eat."

"That sounds good."

"We'll go into the kitchen. Amy, Miss Courtney and I are just going to the kitchen; you can come with us or you can stay there with the toys."

"I'll stay here with the toys," Amy said.

When they were sitting down with tea in front of them, Heather said, "Why don't you have the *boppli* here? It's a bigger house than Aaron's and I can scoot the boys off to one side of the *haus* and you can give birth in the nice big room at the far end of the *haus*—it's the spare room."

"Oh, I'd like that very much. I hope Aaron doesn't mind if I need to take a couple of days off."

"Of course he won't mind if you take all the time you need. He's so much happier and less stressed now that you've come here."

"Is he really?" Courtney studied Heather's face to see if she really meant it.

"*Jah.*"

Courtney took a mouthful of tea pleased she was making a positive difference in Aaron's life. "I hope I don't do anything to disappoint him. I hope all goes well with the birth so I can get directly back into work. Otherwise I don't know what I'm going to do."

"You shouldn't think like that; anything that happens will be *Gott's* will so relax."

"I suppose you're right. I should relax and stop worrying about things but it's hard when so many things have gone wrong for me. And now I've only got myself to rely upon."

"*Jah,* that must be hard. Have you ever thought of getting married again?"

"Maybe I will one day. As you said, it's all *Gott's* will. I don't know how I'd feel about another man. I don't think I'd ever love someone like I loved Mark."

"Have a piece of cake. You've got to keep your strength up."

When Courtney left Heather's place, she felt much better knowing that she and the baby were healthy.

Chapter 13

Let no corrupt communication proceed
out of your mouth,
but that which is good to the use of edifying,
that it may minister grace unto the hearers.
Ephesians 4:29

Now that Courtney's pregnancy had gone past her due date, she woke every day wondering if today was the day she would give birth.

She started to wonder if she'd just get bigger and bigger until she burst. Could her stomach get any bigger than it was now? Courtney prayed every day that the baby would come, but still there was no sign—no little niggles or pains like Heather had said that she might expect.

Everything seemed like the baby was weeks away. From her calculations, she was nearly two weeks overdue. Although Heather told her that as much as three weeks early or late was normal, she couldn't help but be concerned.

Still in her bed, she rolled onto her side and with her hands pushed herself to a sitting position. After she put her legs over the side of the bed, she slipped her feet into her slippers and then drank the rest of the water from the glass on the nightstand. When she stood, she felt water flow down her legs. At first, she thought she'd spilled some water, but she'd drunk it all. Then she realized her water had broken. She still had no pain, but she knew her baby would soon be in her arms. Excitement mixed with fear as she quickly gathered her thoughts.

She pulled on her robe, pushed her hair into her prayer *kapp* and hurried to the main house hoping Aaron was awake. When she pushed the back door open, Aaron was nowhere in sight, but then she heard him coming down the stairs. She stayed put and tried to remain calm.

When he walked into the kitchen and saw her standing there, he said, "What's wrong?"

"The baby!" was all she could say with tears brimming her eyes.

"Now?" he asked.

She nodded. "I think so."

"We'd better get you over to Heather and James' *haus.*"

"I don't think there's any hurry. We could wait for awhile."

"I'm not taking any risks. I'm getting you over there right now. I wouldn't know what to do if things progressed quickly."

She nodded. Her head was in such a spin that she wasn't capable of making the slightest decision.

"Have you got a bag packed like Heather   told you?"

"*Jah.* I've got it just inside the door of the cabin."

"I'll wake Jared and tell him where I'm going. I'll take you to Heather's now and come right back here. Don't worry about the children I'll stay with them today. They won't mind missing a day of *schul.*" He walked a few paces until he was right in front of her and then placed his hands lightly against her arms. "Are you all right?"

"I think so."

"Come and sit on the couch."

"I don't think I should sit." Courtney was worried about messing up the couch.

"You're not going to have the baby right now are you?"

"*Nee* not yet. At least I don't think so."

"Well, stay here; I'll talk to Jared."

Aaron spoke to Jared, and then hurried out to hitch the buggy. Courtney collected her bag from the cabin. Minutes later, they were off to the house where Courtney would give birth.

Courtney glanced at Aaron's concerned face. "You're not the one having the *boppli.*"

His face relaxed into a smile. "I don't like the thought of you going through pain or discomfort and not being able to do anything about it."

"It won't be for long—they tell me. I'm a little bit scared because I haven't done this before. I'd feel better if I knew what to expect."

"Heather will be there to help you." He wiped a tear from his eye.

His concern was of comfort to Courtney. It was nice to have someone in her life who cared so deeply. The last few weeks they'd grown close through their after-dinner conversations once the children had gone to bed.

The buggy came to a halt right at Heather's front door. He rushed around to Courtney and helped her down from the buggy. With his arm through hers, he led her through James and Heather's front door.

Heather had nearly reached the door by the time Aaron had opened it.

"It's time?" Heather asked, standing in her robe and staring at them.

"It is," Aaron answered.

Heather lunged forward and took hold of Courtney's arm.

"I'll leave her in your hands, Heather," Aaron said as Heather led her away. "Wait a minute," Aaron called out. When the women stopped, he walked over to Courtney and put a hand on her shoulder and looked into her eyes and said, "I'll be praying for you, okay?"

She nodded while she noticed Aaron glance at Heather before he looked back at her. He smiled and gave her shoulder a squeeze. She was sure that he wanted to kiss her or hug her, but such a thing would not be appropriate, particularly when Heather was standing right there.

"I'll have James let you know when the baby arrives," Heather said as she made shooing motions to make him leave.

"Okay." He turned and walked out the door.

Heather took Courtney to the room prepared for the birth while asking her what signs she'd had that the baby was coming.

* * *

It was in the evening at fifteen minutes past five that Courtney delivered a baby boy—a healthy baby boy who weighed eight and a half pounds.

Courtney stared down at the baby in her arms—her precious gift from God. She kissed the top of his head. He had a smattering of fine dark hair, and his eyes were dark blue. Courtney was certain that he could focus right away as he stared into her eyes when Heather laid him on her stomach as soon as he was born. He even had strength enough to hold his head up which Heather told her was rare.

Tears streamed down her face, as Courtney was overwhelmed with great love for her child. Heather was there to mop the tears from her face.

"He is just so beautiful," Heather said. "I want another one badly now. Although you could have had a girl since there are too many boys already."

Courtney laughed while not taking her eyes from her baby. "Boy or girl it makes no matter to me. My baby is healthy and well; I couldn't ask for anything more. Mark was taken away from me, but part of him lives on through his baby."

"What are you gonna call him?"

"I'm not certain. I want to choose a strong name. I'll think of something over the next couple of days."

"Do you want to try feeding him?"

"Try? Is it going to be hard?"

"*Nee* it shouldn't be initially, but it might be a bit painful for the first couple of weeks."

Courtney groaned. "More pain?"

"Just a little bit. You could always give him a bottle, but breastfeeding is so much easier, and it's better for the baby and you. So if you can just get past the initial soreness, it'll be worth it."

"Easier sounds good. *Denke* for helping me with everything."

"You don't need to thank me. I'm happy to be here and watch your *boppli* come into the world. Now let's have a go at that feeding."

Chapter 14

And thou shalt love the Lord thy God
with all thine heart,
and with all thy soul, and with all thy might.
Deuteronomy 6:5

Aaron paced up and down waiting for news of the baby. He'd given the children an early dinner and couldn't help horrible fearful thoughts from racing through his mind. What if something went wrong and he lost Courtney?

His agitation caused him to realise that his feelings toward her were more than the feelings he should have toward a nanny. They'd never gone on a date or discussed a relationship, but they'd grown close and he could not deny that he had feelings for her that he never thought he'd have again. Their conversation over the past weeks of discussing the children and the chores had developed into more personal conversations about Courtney's past and how she'd been raised with other orphans within a caring Amish home. He knew her heart and she had captured his, but part of him had held back on doing anything about the way he felt—it was too soon. It was barely more than a year since Ellen had died and it was even less time since Courtney had lost Mark. If God had intended to bless them both with a second love, the love would wait.

Aaron raced to the door when he heard a buggy. He put his hand over his mouth when he saw that it was James, fearing the worst. When he saw James was smiling he ran to him. "Is she all right?" Aaron didn't even notice his children had run out behind him.

"Relax! She's fine and she has a *bu* and he is a big beautiful *boppli*. So I'm told! I'm not allowed to go near them."

"What's his name?" Jared asked.

"They haven't told me that yet."

Aaron said, "Come inside for a while, James."

"I can't, I have to get back to the boys while Heather is looking after Courtney. She might be there for a day or two, or three, or something like that. That's what Heather said to tell you."

"We'll manage. Tell her to take all the time she needs. We're fine here by ourselves, aren't we?" He looked around at the children who nodded, except for Amy who began to cry. He scooped her up into his arms. "What's wrong, Amy?"

"I want Miss Courtney."

He held her tight and rocked her to and fro. "We all do. We all miss her, but she'll be back soon." Aaron looked at his brother who was stared at him and when they locked eyes, James raised one of his eyebrows.

Had James realised that he had feelings for Courtney?

"Can we see the *boppli?*" Ben asked.

"Not in the next couple of days, I'd say. They won't even let me see him."

"We want to see him soon," Jared said.

James laughed. "I'll ask Aunt Heather when is the soonest that you can see him."

"Denke," Jared said.

"Denke for letting us know how they both are,

James."

James got back into his buggy. "You're welcome and I'll ask when you can see the new arrival."

Aaron and the children stayed outside and waved to James until the buggy disappeared. Ushering the children inside, Aaron was filled with guilt. He couldn't shake the feeling that being fond of another woman was being disrespectful to Ellen.

* * *

Two days later, James drove Courtney home. The children ran out to meet her.

"Let me see him first—me first," Jared said pushing everybody else out of the way.

"Don't crowd the *boppli*," Aaron ordered.

Courtney had been looking forward to seeing Aaron and the children and was pleased that Aaron gave her a big smile and asked if she was okay.

When she nodded, he looked at the baby. "He's so lovely, Courtney."

"He is."

Aaron helped her out of the buggy.

"Can I hold him?" Jared asked.

"I'll bring the baby inside and then each of you can have a turn holding him. How does that sound?"

"But you'll have to sit still on the couch," Aaron said.

The children ran into the house.

"Where would you like your bag?" James asked.

Aaron answered for her. "Just put it in her cabin please, James. The door is unlocked."

"Will do, and then I'll head back home."

"*Denke* for everything," Courtney said, "and *denke* for allowing me to keep your wife from you for so long."

"It was lovely having you there, Courtney. You're part of the *familye.*"

Aaron looked at James and James gave him a wink, and then Aaron looked away and took hold of Courtney's arm. "Now let me see this little *bu.*"

Courtney held him up so Aaron could see him.

"He's so small. I forgot how small they are

when they're first born. He's *wunderbaar.*" Aaron blinked back tears.

"You're not going to cry are you?"

He frowned. *"Nee.* I never cry," he said before he sniffed. "He's lovely."

"I know. He's precious."

"We better get you inside." He led her, with the baby in her arms, into the house.

"I hope the birth wasn't too bad."

"It was hard work, but the worst of it was over fairly quickly and then I was nearly back to normal. I feel fine now apart from a few twinges which Heather tells me is completely normal."

"That's good; I was concerned. I really don't want to do without you Courtney." By the time he said that they were in the living room and faced with the three children who were sitting on the couch waiting to hold the baby.

"Me first," Jared said.

Aaron frowned at his oldest son. "Jared, you should let others go first."

"Jah, you should, Jared, but in this case I'll let

you go first because you are the oldest and you've been such a good help to me."

"So have I," Ben said.

"You have been, and so has Amy. All of you have been a really good help but because Jared is the older one he will have first hold."

Jared's face beamed with delight when she placed the baby in his outstretched arms.

"You have to mind his head, Jared."

"It should be all right, I have him wrapped tightly." Courtney kneeled down and stayed close by just in case."

"I will, *Dat*. Will I be his uncle?" Jared asked.

"*Nee,* I think you will be his friend."

"Can I be his friend too?" Amy asked.

"You'll all be his friends and you can teach him lots of things and help him to grow up into a fine young man."

"My turn now," Ben said.

"Okay put out your arms like this." Courtney showed him how to put his arms out. "And you just have to be very careful of his neck."

When Ben had finished his turn, Amy held her hands out and Courtney placed the baby in Amy's arms and stayed close by.

"I love this *boppli*," Amy said, which made everybody giggle. "It's not funny."

"We're not laughing *at* you Amy we're laughing because you're so cute and precious just like this little *boppli*."

Amy smiled.

"Now what about me?" Aaron asked.

"Of course, you can have a hold." When Amy finished her turn, Courtney picked up the baby and handed him to Aaron. Courtney stood back and looked at the sight of a big strong man holding a tiny baby. She wished at that moment that they were all a family. They would make a perfect family and it made sense that she marry Aaron.

She loved Aaron's children and they loved her; Aaron and she had both lost their spouses and even if he wasn't in love with her, surely he could see that it made sense to marry. But maybe he wasn't ready to bring another woman into his heart.

Aaron looked at her and smiled. She smiled back, but inside she hoped she wouldn't get hurt. What if he never developed feelings for her? Worse— what if he developed feelings for her but never proposed. What would she do? She closed her eyes for an instant, holding onto a little bit of hope. He did say a few moments ago that he never wanted to be without her, but did he mean as a woman or as his nanny?

Chapter 15

And be ye kind one to another,
tenderhearted, forgiving one another,
even as God for Christ's sake hath forgiven you.
Ephesians 4:32

Over the next months Courtney kept her feelings for Aaron to herself. She looked forward to the special times at night when she would sit cradling her baby in her arms while listening to him tell his children bedtime stories in front of the fire. When the children were in bed, that was their time alone—Aaron's and her's. Courtney would place her baby in the crib to the side of the room and they would talk over hot tea for hours.

Aaron went to bed after Courtney and baby Gabriel went back to their cabin. Even though she couldn't do as much work as she'd done before the baby had come, his children were looking after her and doing more than they'd ever done.

Jared, Ben, and Amy were receiving life lessons

about taking care of others and that was even more important than having a nanny who fed them and performed chores. What he thought had been a negative at the start had turned into a huge positive. Courtney had changed all of their lives for the better. He noticed a distinct change in the mood of his children since she'd arrived. They had a light on their faces that hadn't been there since they'd lost their mother.

Baby Gabriel was just past eight weeks old and Aaron considered that everything in his life was fine. The only thing that might change that was his sister-in-law, Willa. He had yet to mention to Courtney that Willa and a friend were coming to visit. He'd received a letter from Bessie telling him that they'd be arriving on the Thursday afternoon bus. There was no 'do you mind if we come to stay,' or anything like that, but that was Willa's way. She was a forceful woman—attractive, but forceful. Aaron was surprised that she remained single and he hoped that Willa would not ruin what he had with Courtney. If she saw how he cared for

Courtney she might very well try to ruin things like she'd tried to ruin his relationship with her very own sister, Ellen.

* * *

"My *schweschder*-in-law, Willa, is coming to visit," Aaron announced to Courtney the next day while she was preparing their evening meal.

"*Wunderbaar*! How long since you've seen her?"

"Let me see." He put his hand to his chin with his elbow on the table. "The last time I saw her was at Ellen's funeral."

Courtney nodded. "Was that in the letter you got from Bessie yesterday?"

"*Jah.* I forgot to mention it to you last night." He didn't think it right to tell Courtney that he'd been fond of Willa until he'd met her older sister, whom he then married. "She's bringing a friend."

"When are they arriving?"

"They'll be here on Thursday afternoon."

143

"Gut. How will we accommodate them? Will I put the two younger ones in with Jared and give Willa and her friend a room each?"

"That's exactly what I would've suggested." He looked up at her and gave her a big smile as she poured his *kaffe*. "Sit down with me while the children are quiet. You've got time don't you?"

"Jah, I do. Everything's cooking now."

"I'm surprised that Amy's left you alone. She's usually hanging on to you."

Courtney pulled out a chair and sat down. "She does like to be included in her brothers' games. They're building a farm out of their blocks and they found stones outside that they said look like farm animals."

Aaron chuckled. "Have I told you how you've changed our lives?"

"You did—once or maybe twice." A giggle escaped Courtney's lips.

"I don't know what any of us would do without you now." He stared into her eyes and Courtney looked away. "I'm sorry. I didn't mean to embarrass you, but things that I thought were impossible and would never happen…" He shook his head. "I'm no *gut* with saying how I feel."

She looked into his eyes. "Just say it out loud without thinking."

He took a deep breath and looked into her blue eyes that were staring into his. "I like you, Courtney, more than a nanny or a friend. I know it's early—far too early for either of us, but I wanted to tell you how I feel so there is no misunderstanding between us."

Courtney's eyes had grown wider as she listened to his words and just as she opened her mouth to speak, Amy walked into the kitchen. "Miss Courtney, come see our farm."

"Adults are talking, Amy, and you just interrupted us."

She lowered her head. "Sorry." She looked up at her father. "Excuse me, *Dat.*"

"That's better. You must wait until no one is speaking and then say 'excuse me.'"

"Can I talk now?"

"Go ahead."

"Miss Courtney, will you come see?"

Courtney looked at Aaron who smiled and gave a little nod. "I'd love to see what you've done." Amy took Courtney's hand and led her to the corner of the living room.

Aaron was disappointed that he'd been interrupted. He wanted to know how Courtney felt about him. Even though he sensed she felt the same toward him, there would be no certainty until he heard her words. It was too early to discuss marriage because he still carried pain in his heart over losing Ellen, but if he hadn't told Courtney he was developing feelings for her, she might have taken another job elsewhere. She seemed to receive many letters—what if one of those letters contained a better offer of employment?

He took a mouthful of coffee while listening to the laughter of his children and the words of encouragement from the woman who'd enhanced their lives. He'd already lost one amazing woman and he was going to do everything in his power to hang on to Courtney. Closing his eyes he knew he'd feel great contentment if Courtney and Gabriel were to become part of their family. Rather than the anxiousness that now churned his gut with knowing she could leave at any time, he knew in his heart he'd feel a sense of peace and fulfillment if they merged their households. Even though his head told him it was too soon, a part of him longed to care for Courtney and Gabriel as part of his family.

Aaron walked over to the coffee pot and poured himself another coffee and one for Courtney, hoping she'd come back and finish their conversation.

Courtney listened while Jared, Ben, and Amy told her all about their model farm and what animals they had. Each of them had separate animals that they kept in three barns all built from wooden blocks.

"You've all done so well," she said when they finished telling her about their creation.

"Do you want to stay and play with us?" Ben asked.

"Any other time I would, but I must go back to the kitchen and speak to your *vadder* before dinner is ready. Ten more minutes of play and you'll have to wash up for the evening meal. Jared, you can watch the time."

Jared glanced up at the clock on the mantel and nodded.

"Gut." Courtney got off the blanket on the floor where they had spread out their blocks. Aaron liked her and she liked him. What was to stop them from taking their relationship further? If they did and things didn't work out as they both hoped, she'd have to find work elsewhere. It wasn't a good idea to jeopardize her job. She'd have to tell him she'd prefer things remained the same between them.

When she stepped back into the kitchen, he looked up. "There you are. I'm glad to see they let you go." He chuckled. "I've poured you some kaffe."

"Is that your second cup?" When he nodded, she added, "I hope you'll still have room for dinner." She sat in front of her coffee and took a sip.

"Denke."

"About what I was saying before you were stolen away."

She put the cup down and stared into his eyes to feel her heart melt and her defenses against him slide away. "Yes?"

"Do you feel the same way as I?"

All she could do was nod. Her steely reserve was no match for the way he made her feel.

He reached out across the table and took her hand in his. A sense of relief washed over her as though her life would never be the same. Aaron was one of the nicest, kindest men she'd ever known and she felt completely at home with him and his children as though this is what God had planned for both of them. They were perfect for one another. They'd both lost their spouses with whom they'd each had children. Who better to understand how much she missed her husband than someone who'd loved and also lost?

The children interrupted them by walking through the kitchen to get to the washroom where they would wash their hands before dinner.

He let go of her hand but not before giving her a special smile.

"I better get dinner finished and when the children have washed their hands, they can set the table."

"You've got everyone organized," Aaron said.

"I will have, if Gabriel sleeps through the meal."

Throughout the meal that night there was a quiet understanding between Aaron and Courtney. Courtney felt her stomach lurch every time they caught each other's eyes.

As soon as dinner was over, Gabriel woke. Courtney fed him in the privacy of Jared's bedroom while Jared organized Ben and Amy to clean the kitchen and do the dishes. While Courtney was breastfeeding, she could hear the children talking as they cleared the dishes and filled the sink with water. She'd taken a big risk to keep her pregnancy a secret when she'd accepted the job as nanny, but everything had worked out perfectly. There had been bumps along the road at the beginning, but now those snags were behind her.

Chapter 16

Commit thy works unto the Lord,
and thy thoughts shall be established.
Proverbs 16:3

"If you don't mind looking after the children, I'll go and collect Willa and her friend and bring them back here."

"Okay."

"Have you organized their bedrooms?"

"Jah, I've moved Ben and Amy into Jared's room. I've made the beds up and everything is ready for them." Courtney had been looking forward to some new female company.

"Denke, Courtney. I don't know what I would ever do without you." He flashed her a bright smile that made her heart leap. "You were right when you said that you could do everything. You're quite a remarkable woman and you've been wonderful with the children."

Courtney giggled.

"I mean it. You've changed my life completely. I can enjoy the children when I come home instead of doing more work. I hope you stay with us forever."

"Forever's a long time." Courtney could've suggested a way she could stay with them forever but she didn't. Maybe one day he'd want her to stay around for a different reason. Her secret hope was that one day they would marry and they could be a real family.

"I'll have to find a way to make you stay. But right now I've got to collect Willa and her friend."

After she stood with the children and watched Aaron drive away in his buggy, she had the children help her with getting the dinner cooked. Jared complained that he shouldn't have to do women's work and wanted to do boys' work. Courtney explained to him that he could do both just like his father had to do both before she came along.

It was about an hour later that they heard the buggy return. The children ran from the kitchen and Courtney wasn't far behind them. Courtney stopped at the front door and watched an attractive woman step down from the buggy. Then another woman stood alongside her. The one doing all the talking and pointing to things was obviously Willa. On closer scrutiny, Courtney saw Willa was slim with a pretty face and a slightly upturned nose.

The children were standing in a row in front of Courtney while Gabriel was fast asleep in the house.

Willa stepped forward. "Don't you remember your Aunty Willa?

"Nee," Jared said which caused Ben and Amy to giggle.

After Willa had leaned down and hugged the three children, she looked up at Courtney. "And you must be Candice?"

"I'm Courtney," Courtney said, accepting a warm hug from Willa while Beth giggled.

"Hello, Courtney. I'm Beth," Beth said giving Courtney a nod.

"Hello, Beth."

"I meant to say Courtney; those two names are so similar—both are common names." Willa glanced over at Aaron who was tending to the horse and then looked back at Courtney. "We are quite tired and hungry from the journey. Do you have food prepared?"

"Dinner will be ready in half an hour. Would you like something before that? I can fix you some tea and something to eat right now if you're really hungry."

"We can wait," Willa said in a bored tone. "Can you show us where we'll be sleeping?"

"Of course, come inside." Once they were inside, Courtney walked down the hallway with the two women following. "Your rooms are down this way. I've fixed you a room each."

"Where do the children sleep?" Willa asked.

"They're all bunking down in Jared's room." Courtney pointed behind her to the enclosed porch, which was Jared's room.

As Courtney continued to lead the way, she asked Willa. "Have you been here before?"

"*Jah.* I have been here many times to visit. How long have you been here?"

"I've been here for quite a few months now."

"And where do you stay?" Beth asked.

"I'm staying in the cabin next door. It's very close to the *haus.*"

"I see," said Willa. "And Aaron tells me you have a *boppli?*"

"*Jah,* I do. He's four months old."

"My *mudder* is trying to tell Aaron to move closer to the *familye.* You wouldn't try to stop him from doing that would you, Courtney?"

"Nee, of course, not. Why would I do that?"

"You must make him see that he should move back to Lancaster County to be closer to the people who care about him."

"I can't make him do anything. He has his own mind; I'm only the nanny."

Willa looked her up and down. "I know that's all you are and all you'll ever be to him, but if you care about his *kinner* at all, you'll do your best to persuade him. Don't you want what's best for him?"

"I do, Willa. He's made a life for himself   here

and he seems to be happy."

"He'll be happy anywhere and the children will be happier if they have more children to play with."

"They have their cousins just down the road and they see them nearly every day."

"Willa's only trying to help, Courtney," Beth said.

Courtney stared at Beth. "I know that, but sometimes people just have to step back and trust that other people know what's best for themselves. We can't control others, we can only make decisions for ourselves."

"And why are you trying to make him stay, then?" Willa asked placing her hands on her hips and tilting her chin toward the ceiling.

"I'm not making him do anything. I've never had one conversation with him about staying here or leaving." Courtney bit the inside of her lip hoping that was true. In their many conversations something might have come up along those lines at some stage.

"Just by being here you're making it easier for

him to stay."

"Before I came here, Heather was looking after them. It didn't make him leave when he had no one living here minding the children."

"Don't say anymore, Willa. She doesn't understand what you mean."

"You're right, Beth." Willa stepped into the room. "Is this where I'm staying?"

"*Jah,* and Beth, you're right across the hallway. The rooms aren't big but I hope you'll be comfortable."

Willa spun around and stared at Courtney. "You think it's a small *haus?*"

"*Jah,* much smaller than most of the homes in Ohio and Lancaster County."

"Well, *denke,* Courtney. I'm sure we'll be comfortable in the tiny rooms in the small *haus.*"

"*Gut,* well then, I'll go and put the pot on for some *kaffe* while you both get settled in."

"*Denke,* Courtney," Willa called out before Beth echoed the same.

Courtney walked away and hurried to check how

the children were getting along minding her baby whom she'd left in the kitchen in his crib.

"We've set the table for dinner," Jared said pleased with himself.

"Jared, that looks *wunderbaar*. You've all done so well; you're such good helpers."

"Gabriel is still asleep," Amy said as Courtney peered into the small crib.

"*Denke,* for watching him. He's a blessed *boppli* to have all of you watching over him as he sleeps."

Aaron walked in the back door. "Where are the visitors?" he whispered.

"They're getting settled in their rooms."

"Did they say how long they're staying?"

Courtney shook her head and seeing her response, Aaron pulled a face.

"Just finish at your usual time tonight, Courtney, unless you'd like to stay here and talk with us. What I mean to say is that they'll probably stay up late and I don't want you to feel obligated to stay when you've got the *boppli* to look after. There's no reason why both of us should miss out on sleep."

"Okay, *denke.*" Courtney turned her back on him to check the dinner while wondering if he wanted to talk to the two women alone. Did he fancy one of them? Maybe she would be able to tell over dinner. Either way, she'd make herself scarce as soon as the children were in bed and the after-dinner cleanup was completed.

Courtney had to wake her baby up to feed him before dinner. When the baby had been fed, changed and settled back in his crib, there was still no sign of Willa or Beth. With dinner being ready, Courtney sent Jared in to fetch them.

Chapter 17

Study to shew thyself approved unto God,
a workman that needeth not to be ashamed,
rightly dividing the word of truth.
2 Timothy 2:15

Once they were sitting around the table, they all closed their eyes and said their silent prayer of thanks for the food.

Courtney dished the food onto the children's plates while Aaron passed the bowls of food to the two guests.

"Courtney, why do you have the children at the same table as the adults?"

"That's my decision," Aaron said. "It's got nothing to do with Courtney."

"I like it. I think it's nice for the children to sit up and eat with the adults rather than sit at their own table. That way, they can be taught the proper table manners. Who knows what they would do left to their own ways?"

"It's a lovely *haus* you have here, Aaron. Courtney thinks it's too small, but we both told her it's a good size."

Courtney winced and then didn't know how to respond to the comment. It was a small house in comparison with others, but the way Willa had said it made it sound like she'd been speaking in a derogatory manner about Aaron's house. All she could do was spoon food on her plate while avoiding eye contact with anyone.

"It is a small house and I could've extended it, but chose to build a cabin for a nanny instead."

"Did you hear that, Courtney? If you hadn't come then he could've made this house bigger," Beth said.

"*Jah,* I heard what he said. And I don't think this house is too small, it's smaller than some, that's all."

"I think it's a beautiful *haus,*" Willa said, placing a small hand on Aaron's wrist and flashing him a smile.

"*Denke,* Willa. I'll probably need a bigger *haus*

sometime, but right now this one suits us fine. It's all we need."

Courtney glanced up at him hoping he'd give her a reassuring smile or a look to let her know that 'us' included her and Gabriel. He didn't look at her.

"*Dat* says a smaller *haus* is warmer. If we had a bigger one we'd need two fireplaces," Jared said to Willa.

"When I was a child, I wasn't allowed to speak to adults at the dinner table unless one of them spoke to me."

Jared's gaze dropped to his dinner plate and he said no more.

"I encourage my children to talk over dinner. We tell each other about our day and what we each did. There's only been the four of us for some time until we were blessed with Courtney, and of course, young Gabriel."

Courtney's body flooded with warmth when Aaron looked at her and smiled. The smile they exchanged wasn't lost on Willa who, Courtney noticed, moved uncomfortably in her chair.

"Did the children cook the dinner?" Beth asked.

"*Nee*, I cooked it, but they always help me."

"Isn't it hard for you to do your job with a *boppli?*" Beth had emphasized the word, 'job.'

"I admit I was stressed when I found out that Courtney would soon be giving birth, but I must say it's worked out well. Courtney and Gabriel are like part of the *familye.*"

"As long as she's doing her job that's all you can ask for," Willa said.

Aaron cleared his throat. "The food is *wunderbaar* as usual, Courtney."

"*Denke,* Aaron."

"*Jah,* Courtney it is *gut,*" Willa agreed.

"I have *wunderbaar* helpers."

"Ellen was such a great cook." Willa's comment was greeted with a hush. The silence lasted until everyone had nearly finished what was on their plates.

"Would anyone like more? There's plenty left," Courtney said, purely to break the silence.

Aaron was the only person who had seconds.

Dessert was had without incident or careless comments. Courtney planned to leave for her cabin as soon as she could.

She put the children to bed, and while Aaron and his two guests were talking in the living room, Courtney cleaned the kitchen and washed up.

"Do you want any help in here?"

Courtney turned away from the sudsy dishes in the sink to see Willa. *"Nee, denke.* I'm fine."

"I'll dry the dishes. How's that?"

"You don't need to."

"I know I don't, but I will."

"Okay."

Courtney passed her a tea towel. After she was halfway through the dishes, Willa said, "Did you know how angry Aaron was when you arrived here and he learned you were expecting?"

She studied Willa's face. "How do you know?"

"He wrote to Bessie."

Courtney looked into the dish suds. He always wrote to Bessie and confided in her. "What did he say?"

"He said that he'll see how you work out and that he wasn't happy. Bessie was shocked too when she found out you were keeping your pregnancy a secret. She said it put her in a bad light for recommending you to her nephew."

"I feel terrible."

Willa placed the tea towel down. "Liars are always found out."

Courtney looked away from her and continued scrubbing the dishes. She was a liar, no matter what excuse she made for herself. Just because she knew she could do the job with a baby was no reason to deceive people, but if she hadn't would she be here now? Surely what she'd done was only for the very best reasons. It was a small lie—if you could call withholding information a lie at all.

"Nothing to say?"

Courtney looked up shocked. *"Nee.* Do I need to answer to you?"

Willa's jaw dropped open and her face changed into a scowl. "I've never had anyone be so rude to me. It's you who is in the wrong. You came here under false pretences and now you're trying to steal Aaron away and make him marry you." Her words were low and hissed.

"I'm doing no such thing. Really I'm not," Courtney said.

"I know what you're doing and I'm not leaving here until Aaron knows exactly what sort of person you are." Willa turned on her heel and stomped out of the kitchen.

As soon as she was gone, Aaron came in and said, "I'll put the pot on for some hot tea."

"Nee, Aaron you go back and talk to your guests. I'll bring some tea out when it's ready." Courtney's tone was firm. She hoped that he wouldn't see she was upset.

"Are you certain? I don't mind."

"Nee. It's fine and as soon as I do that I'll go, if that's okay."

"Go whenever you like." Aaron walked out of the kitchen but not before he peeped into Gabriel's crib.

A tear trickled down Courtney's face while she wondered if she should move on. Willa was going to do her best to make her life miserable—that was plain to see. The longer Willa and her friend stayed there, the longer the children would be sleeping in the one room, which would ruin their nightly bedtime routine. Aaron would feel he had to entertain the guests rather than telling the children their nightly bedtime stories.

By the time the pot boiled, Courtney had washed and dried all the dishes from the evening meal. She placed the tea on a tray and took it out to the living room.

"Denke, Courtney, you're such a hard-worker." Willa stared at the tray once Courtney placed it on the coffee table. *"Ach nee.* I wanted *kaffe."*

"That was my fault," Aaron said, "I asked Courtney for hot tea."

"It's no trouble to fix *kaffe."* Courtney said right before her baby began to cry.

"You go home, Courtney. You've done more than enough for one day. You must be exhausted."

"Nee, I'm okay."

"Aaron's right, Courtney. Your *boppli* needs you. Beth and I will look after Aaron."

Courtney turned and walked into the kitchen. She picked up her baby and his bag of diapers and spare clothes and headed to the front door. "Well, *gut nacht."* Without waiting for a reply she headed to her cabin hoping that no one saw how upset she was.

Chapter 18

Commit thy way unto the Lord;
trust also in him; and he shall bring it to pass.
Psalm 37:5

Aaron knew there was something wrong with Courtney. She didn't even look at him when she'd left. Normally he liked to say goodnight to her baby, even if the baby was asleep and tonight he was well and truly awake. It was so unlike her to rush out the door like that.

He walked into the kitchen and saw that Courtney had left the kitchen in a messy state and not how she normally would have left it. *She must've been in a hurry.* There were little things she always did that remained undone—wipe the oven surface down, and lay out the breakfast dishes ready for the morning—it was clear she'd left in a hurry.

Willa walked up behind him. "I can fix my own *kaffe,* Aaron. You don't have to do it."

"It's no trouble."

Willa grabbed his hand and then with her other hand took the coffee pot out of his hands. Willa's looks reminded him very much of Ellen; they both had clear creamy skin and bright green eyes. It was nice to have someone in the house who'd been so close to his late wife.

He pulled his hand away when he realized Willa was holding it a little too long. "I'll let you do it, then."

Willa filled the pot with water. "Bessie told me you're not happy with Courtney."

Aaron scratched his head. "She got the letter I wrote right after Courtney arrived. I was a little shocked she arrived when she was so close to giving birth. I never meant to send the letter. It was sent accidently."

"How can you send a letter accidently?"

"It's a long story. It doesn't matter now. I'm more than happy with Courtney. All of us are so happy she's here. I don't know what we'd ever do if she left."

"What will you do when she leaves?"

He chuckled. "We'll just have to hope she never leaves."

"She didn't tell you?"

"Tell me what?"

"Nothing. Never mind. Pretend I didn't say anything."

"Did she tell you something about leaving? Is she leaving?"

"I'm not saying a thing, Aaron. You should know if someone deceives you once they'll deceive you twice."

Aaron pulled out a chair from under the dining table and sat down heavily. Was Willa right? If Courtney had thought nothing of keeping something so important as a pregnancy from both him and Bessie, how could he trust her completely? By the sounds of things, Courtney had told Willa she had plans to leave and she'd never mentioned anything to him—not even when he'd told her that he was developing serious feelings.

"That's no good. I don't want her to leave and the children will be devastated. It will be like   losing their *mudder* all over again. And they've become attached to little Gabriel."

Willa sat next to him and put her hand over his. "Sometimes when one door closes another opens. When you lose something, you gain another thing. If Courtney leaves, I might be able to stay on."

Even without her offer to stay, it was the second time that night that she'd come close, inappropriately close, and the third time she had put her hand on him. He knew without a doubt that she was fond of him. He turned and looked at her and she stared into his eyes and moved her head a little closer while her gaze dropped to his lips. *She wants me to kiss her.* Willa was an attractive woman, but things were moving much too quickly. Besides she was Ellen's *schweschder,* which made everything more awkward. A host of thoughts ran through his mind. If he did marry a second time, the children would have a mother and he'd have a woman to love and to care for.

"I've always liked you, Aaron." She fluttered her lashes at him.

He shook his head. "It feels wrong. You're Ellen's *schweschder.*"

"Ellen has gone now and she's never coming back. Don't your *kinner* deserve to have a *mudder* and be raised properly? I know Courtney is nice and everything, but she'll never love your *kinner* the way she loves her *boppli.*"

"Courtney just works for us. I don't require her to love my *kinner* more than she loves her own."

"You don't think she wants more?"

"*Nee,* I don't."

She wrapped her fingers around his hand and leaned closer.

He leaned back. "I think the pot is boiling."

She turned her head toward the stove and got up from the table. "Think about what I said," she whispered glancing back at him. "You don't have to pay a nanny when you can marry again."

Aaron knew exactly what she meant. She was saying he could marry her—Willa was as good as throwing herself at him.

"I hear you," he said hoping that would be the

end of their conversation. "We better get back to Beth. It's been rude to leave her alone for so long."

"She won't mind."

"What can I do to help?" he asked standing up.

"Nothing. You go out and talk to Beth. I'll be out in a minute."

Aaron glanced at the clock in the kitchen before he went out. It was approaching eight and that was around the time he got ready for bed. He hoped the ladies wouldn't talk for too long.

* * *

Courtney fed her baby as soon as she got back to the cabin. Before the dinner, she had only given him a small feeding to tide him over until she got back to her cabin.

She stared down at Gabriel as he suckled and he looked at her and smiled.

Courtney giggled. "You're such a beautiful *bu.* What would I do without you?"

Willa had planted a seed in her mind about

leaving. She'd have to leave Aaron and the children one day if he married someone else—someone who wasn't her.

"Perhaps Willa has plans of becoming his wife?" she said to Gabriel who immediately stopped sucking and looked at her. *"Jah,* you think so too, don't you?"

Gabriel smiled again.

"I know it's true, but what do I do? Every time I think that my life is going fine, something always comes up to ruin things. My mistake was that I grew fond of Aaron. I shouldn't have imagined us as husband and wife; that must not be in *Gott's* plans for our lives, Gabriel."

This time, her baby ignored her—not even looking up. "You don't agree?" She glanced at the clock on the mantle. "I know it to be true. I never thought I'd have feelings for another man other than your *vadder* and here I am falling in love with the first man who gives me a job. What a lovely man he is, though. So kind and thoughtful—so gentle in heart and mind. My body is tingling now just thinking about him."

She looked down to see Gabriel was nearly asleep.

"Just like your *vadder*. He never listened too much when I talked either." All of a sudden her stomach churned just the way it had when she'd first met Mark. When she'd wait for him to take her on their frequent buggy rides, her stomach would churn, wondering if he liked her as much as she liked him.

She didn't like the feeling of angst she had and couldn't help thinking the worst thing that could happen was that he'd grow fond of Willa, his late wife's sister.

Courtney placed Gabriel upright and patted him on his back, glad that she'd already changed his diaper before she'd fed him. He didn't wake so she placed him in his crib by her bedside.

When she turned off the gas lamp, she walked to the window where she could see the main house. The lights were still on in the living room and none were on in the bedrooms.

"They're still talking," she murmured to herself. "Aaron will be tired tomorrow if he doesn't get some sleep soon."

Courtney lit the lamp again, grabbed her robe and headed to the tiny bathroom off from the bedroom. After she'd bathed she looked again at the house to see that the light was still blazing in the living room. She leaned down and kissed her baby softly on the top of his head, and with a sigh, she slipped between the covers and buried her head in the pillow.

All evening she'd been trying to bury her annoyance at the comments by Willa and her friend and trying not to be aggravated by them, but now all their comments were echoing in her ears.

After a few minutes of working out what exactly was upsetting her, she realized it wasn't Willa and it wasn't Beth. What was upsetting her was the feeling that she wasn't in control of her life. She'd had no control over Mark dying and just when she felt she had a comfortable life again, it looked like the rug was going to be swiftly pulled from under her.

"Give me patience please, *Gott.*" She switched off the gas lamp on the nightstand, closed her eyes and said her usually nightly prayers.

"If you'll excuse me, ladies, I'll have to say goodnight. I have to get up and start work early. It slipped my mind to mention it to Courtney, but you can have the use of the buggy tomorrow as soon as Courtney drops the boys to Heather's *haus* for *schul.*"

"And what time do you finish work?"

"Around dark, sometimes earlier."

"I hope you won't be working all the time."

He rose to his feet. "I'm not in a position to take time off. I won't be working on Sunday."

Willa pouted. "No one works on Sunday. Can't you take just a little time off seeing that we've come all this way?"

"I'll have to see what I can do, but it won't be tomorrow. *Gut nacht.*" After they said goodnight to him, Aaron headed up the stairs to his bedroom. He hoped he wasn't being rude. If Ellen were still alive, she would've stayed talking to their guests. But if Ellen had been alive Willa wouldn't have approached him so tenderly in the kitchen. Even though his wife was no longer around, he still felt that what Willa did was uncomfortable. He'd given her no indication he was fond of her. He closed his bedroom door, pleased to be away from the mindless chatter of Willa and Beth.

Chapter 19

Be strong and of a good courage,
fear not, nor be afraid of them:
for the LORD thy God,
he it is that doth go with thee;
he will not fail thee, nor forsake thee.
Deuteronomy 31:6

Courtney woke when she heard her baby cry. She got out of bed, picked Gabriel up, and took him back to her bed where she fed him. Through her partly opened curtains she saw it was still dark outside so she knew she wasn't late. When Gabriel finished his feeding, she changed his diaper and it was then that she looked at the clock to see she was running fifteen minutes late—it was six fifteen. Normally she would've had Aaron's breakfast cooking by now.

She pulled her nightgown off and replaced it with a yellow dress. After she tied her apron on, she pushed her hair under her *kapp* without taking the time to braid it. Then she wrapped Gabriel in a warm blanket and hurried to the house.

When she pushed the back door open she saw light in the kitchen and smelled the breakfast cooking. Walking further inside, she saw Willa had taken over and was standing in front of the stove. Aaron was sitting at the table drinking from a coffee mug.

Words tumbled out of her mouth. *"Ach,* I'm so sorry I overslept."

Willa spun around to look at her just as Aaron said, "It was a late night for all of us."

"I can't see a man go out to do a full day's work without a good meal in his stomach."

"Denke for starting breakfast, Willa." Courtney placed her baby in the crib off to the side of the kitchen.

Willa smiled. "I'm pleased to help."

Courtney walked up beside Willa. "Would you like to sit down and talk to Aaron while I finish the cooking?"

Willa looked at her as though she'd said

something   rude. *"Nee.* I'll finish what I started. That's what women do—some women."

Courtney took a step back not knowing what Willa meant, but guessing that it was a personal jab at her.

Aaron stood up. "Sit down, Courtney. I'll get you some coffee."

"I can get it," Courtney said.

"Nee, Courtney, allow me to do one little thing for you for once."

Courtney gave a little giggle, and said, "Okay as long as it's just this once."

"Scrambled egg and bacon okay for you, Courtney?" Willa asked just as Aaron placed a full cup of coffee in front of Courtney.

Raising her eyebrows in surprise at the gesture, Courtney said, *"Denke,"* to Aaron, and then to Willa, *"Jah* please, Willa. That'd be fine. It's nice to have breakfast cooked for me."

"You should teach the children to cook the breakfast," Willa said. "Well, perhaps just Amy."

Courtney frowned. She didn't want the boys

to think they shouldn't learn to cook. "She's too young to be near a stove and she doesn't wake early enough."

Willa glanced over at her. "Oh Courtney, you seem to have an answer for everything. It's too early in the morning to listen to excuses."

Courtney looked into her coffee and took a sip. She could feel Aaron looking at her but didn't look up in case he was giving her a look of disapproval. "Do you have plans for the day, Willa?" Courtney hoped that Willa and Beth had plans that would take them out of the house; otherwise she didn't know how she would cope with their digging remarks.

Aaron cut in, "I was going to mention to you that I offered the use of the buggy to Beth and Willa after you take Ben and Jared to *schul.*"

"That's a wonderful idea. There are so many pretty things to see around here."

"How would we know where they are unless we have a guide?" Willa dished the eggs and bacon onto three plates. After she placed them on the table, she sat down and asked, "Won't you come with us, Courtney?"

"Um… I do have to bake bread. You've probably noticed that we've run out."

"*Jah,* I did. I wasn't going to say anything about that, but I certainly noticed that there was no fresh bread. When I get married, my husband will wake to the smell of fresh bread cooking."

"He'll be a very blessed man," Aaron said smiling at Willa.

Courtney couldn't help being upset that Willa had come to stay. Why couldn't she have stayed right where she was? Aaron was just beginning to open up about his feelings and now Willa could possibly ruin their hopes of any kind of future together.

"I think it takes more than bread to keep a man happy." Courtney couldn't keep quiet. Irritation had driven her so much that she had to say something.

Willa looked up from her breakfast and glared at Courtney. "Forgive me, Courtney. You'd know because you've been married before. I wouldn't know things like that because I've never had the benefit of experience that an older woman has had."

Courtney ate her breakfast in silence. There was no point in saying more. If Aaron was swayed by the attractive, Willa, he was not the man for her.

"I'm sure Courtney would love to show you around normally, but she does have many things to do around here. And she hasn't had much time to see many things since her arrival. I'm afraid between me and the children she's been kept busy."

"Yes, not to mention her own little unexpected arrival."

"Gabriel has been a blessing to all of us. He has a special place in our hearts," Aaron replied.

Courtney looked at Aaron and they exchanged smiles.

Willa leaned toward Aaron. "Well, aren't you a sweet man, Aaron. It's endearing to find a man who loves babies so much when they are no relation to him whatsoever."

The woman was testing Courtney's patience

with every word that she spoke.

"I'll leave the both of you to work it out about the use of the buggy." Aaron put the last forkful of food into his mouth. When he finished he said, "The breakfast was splendid."

"It would've been nicer if we had fresh bread to go with it," Willa added.

"*Nee,* we don't need to eat bread every day. One day without it will make no difference." Aaron stood up. "If you'll both excuse me, I'll get going."

"Have a lovely day at work, Aaron. I'll make sure you have a *wunderbaar* meal waiting for you when you get home."

"That's nice of you, Willa, but Courtney's sees to that. Why don't you relax and enjoy yourself while you're here?"

"*Denke,* I might do that."

Willa was smiling so smugly at Aaron that Courtney wanted to smack the smile right off her face. Courtney took stock of herself and bit down hard on her lip—physical violence, or any kind of violence, was not the Amish way. She'd never been tested the way that Willa was testing her right now.

"Bye, Courtney."

Courtney turned to look at Aaron near the back door. "Bye. Have a *gut* day."

"I will." Aaron pulled on his work boots and walked out the door.

"Well, *denke* for this lovely breakfast, Willa. It's nice eating a meal I didn't have to cook."

"Does Aaron work you too hard?" Willa cupped her chin in her hands with her elbows on the table, appearing to be concerned.

Courtney knew she was only asking so she could make trouble by twisting whatever answer she gave her. "I can't complain about anything. The children are *wunderbaar* and Aaron is just perfect to work for. I'm so blessed to be here."

Willa looked disappointed by her answer.

"Now you sit there and I'll fix the dishes."

"Now? Don't you wait for the children to eat so you don't waste so much water? If you do two washes it'll waste twice as much water."

"I usually only do one wash," Courtney said.

"Why should today be different, then?"

Courtney sighed. How could she tell the woman she was trying to be nice to her but she was making it awfully hard? "It's just that I didn't want you to do it. I can do all the work while you and Beth relax and enjoy your vacation."

"That's very kind of you. I'm used to pitching in and helping wherever I am—even when I'm not at home."

"Do you live with your parents?"

"I do. I nearly got married once but that didn't work out."

Now Courtney felt bad for being so cross with her. By the expression on Willa's face she appeared genuinely sad that the marriage hadn't taken place. Willa was old to have never married; Courtney guessed her to be maybe twenty six. She was an attractive woman, but her friend, Beth, was not so attractive.

"I'm sorry to hear that. That must have been disappointing."

Willa nodded. "It truly was. He married someone

else instead of me."

"Oh."

"I guess it wasn't meant to be—and all that."

"It's hard to hear that when something sad happens."

Willa giggled. "I did hear that a lot at the time. Now I can see why it all happened the way it did."

"That's good. So did you realize he wasn't the right man for you?" Courtney asked.

Willa's green eyes sparkled with light. "Something like that."

Courtney wasn't sure what she meant but at least she was feeling a little more kindly toward her and all thoughts of hitting her had left. How could she remain mad at a woman who'd known the pain of love that had being taken away from her?

"And what about you, Courtney?"

"In what way?"

"What plans do you and Gabriel have for the rest of your lives?"

"I'd say that's in *Gott's* hands."

"Would you marry again?"

192

"If *Gott* wills it." Courtney noticed a flicker of agitation on Willa's face in reaction to her answers. She figured if she kept talking about God then Willa had little chance of running off to Aaron and reporting a twisted representation of what she'd said.

Chapter 20

But they that wait upon the LORD shall
renew their strength;
they shall mount up with wings as eagles;
they shall run, and not be weary;
and they shall walk, and not faint.
Isaiah 40:31

W hen Aaron got home that evening he came after having received bad news. Courtney knew something was wrong as soon as she saw his face.

"What is it, Aaron?"

"I'm afraid it's Bessie." He walked further into the house and sat down with Courtney and the two visitors. The children were playing on the floor and Gabriel was asleep in the crib.

"Is she ill?" Willa asked.

"She's gone home."

Willa immediately put her head between her hands and sobbed. Beth rubbed her on her back.

"When is the funeral?" Beth asked.

"Tuesday. I must go, Courtney."

"Jah, of course you must. I'll mind the children. How did she die?"

"In her sleep. She didn't suffer."

Willa looked up. "Beth and I must go too. Don't you want to go, Courtney?"

"Jah, but it's hard with the *boppli* and the children."

"Didn't you know her?" Beth asked.

"Courtney knew Bessie. Bessie recommended her for the job as nanny."

"I remember that," Willa said. "She showed me a letter you wrote to her Aaron. The letter you sent right after Courtney got here."

Courtney noticed Aaron didn't like Willa mentioning the letter, which caused Courtney to wonder what was in it. Willa's comment made Courtney's stomach churn like it had when Courtney had first arrived at Aaron's house.

"Are you okay, Willa? I didn't know you knew Bessie that well," Aaron said.

Looking up with tears in her eyes, she said. "I stayed with her for a few weeks a couple of years back."

"She was a kind woman," he said.

"I'll come to the funeral with you," Willa said.

"Are you cutting your stay here short?" Courtney asked hoping she hadn't sounded too anxious to hear the word 'yes.'

"I'm too upset to know what I'm doing, Courtney."

"We could all go," Courtney suggested, only so she could keep her eye on Willa.

"*Nee,* there's no need to disrupt the children like that. I'll go, if you don't mind looking after the children by yourself for a week or so, Courtney?" Aaron asked. "James has already decided he needs to stay here to manage the farm, so he and Heather will be able to help you if you need anything."

"Of course. I don't mind, Aaron, that will be fine."

"You're such a good worker," Beth said to Courtney.

Courtney didn't reply.

Aaron, Willa, and Beth went to James' house to use the phone in his barn to organize bus tickets. Courtney couldn't help being worried that he would be away from her and in close proximity to Willa who was trying to win him over.

* * *

The bus trip with Willa and Beth was a nightmare. Willa abandoned her friend to sit next to Aaron. All the way to Lancaster County she spoke of marriage and how she desperately wanted to be a mother. She was throwing herself at him and he knew it. He was upset that she hadn't brought all her luggage with her, which meant that she would be going back with him and staying longer at his house. He'd tried to tell Willa to sit with Beth, that he preferred to be alone, but she failed to take the hint. After a while her voice was grating on his nerves.

* * *

It was the Saturday that Aaron, Willa and Beth had left to go back to Lancaster County and Courtney needed someone to talk to. She bundled the children into the buggy and headed off to visit Heather. The children were excited about playing with their cousins.

As soon as the buggy was close to the house, James and Heather's children ran outside to greet Aaron's children. Courtney stopped the buggy to let them out and then she saw Heather waving from the doorway.

"Great minds think alike," Heather called out.

"What do you mean?"

"I just told the boys that we'd go over and visit you."

Courtney laughed as she tied up the reins of the buggy to the post. Heather reached into the buggy and got Gabriel out.

"Stop growing, Gabriel. You're growing too fast."

"That's what everyone says, but I can't see him growing. I only notice that he's growing out of his clothes."

"Come inside. I've got plenty of boys' clothes. I'll get them down from the attic. I've kept all their baby clothes."

"You've already given me so much."

"There's more," Heather said, "and you can just give them back when he's outgrown them."

When they were sitting down in the kitchen, away from the noisy children playing in the living room, Heather asked, "Are you missing Aaron already."

Courtney looked at Heather to see if she knew her secret. "Am I that obvious?"

"I've known for a while."

"Oh. I thought that with Willa visiting I might learn a little of Ellen and what she was like, but Willa's not easy to talk with."

Heather scoffed. "I suppose you wouldn't know would you?"

"Know what?"

"Aaron and Willa once dated."

Courtney's jaw dropped open. "He never mentioned anything."

"It probably was nothing to him. It was just once or twice and then he met Willa's sister, Ellen."

"And Willa was angry about that?"

"Ach jah! Willa was extremely angry and accused Ellen of stealing him from her. The two women didn't talk for years. In a matter of months after they met, Ellen and Aaron were married.*"

"So Ellen hadn't always lived in Lancaster?"

"Nee. The *familye* moved there from somewhere else. I'm not certain where from."

"I suppose that explains Willa's attitude to me. She wasn't very nice at all."

"She's trying to get him back."

Courtney recalled a conversation she'd had recently with Willa where she said she'd nearly gotten married—could she have meant she'd nearly gotten married to Aaron? "Do you think Aaron likes her?"

Heather shook her head. "Not one little bit. That's what I think anyway."

"Gut!"

The two women giggled.

Chapter 21

And now abideth faith, hope,
charity, these three;
but the greatest of these is charity.
1 Corinthians 13:13

It was a week and a half later that Heather visited Courtney and informed her that Aaron had phoned for James to collect him from the bus station.

"Come in, Heather."

"Nee, I've just driven here to tell you that, and I must get home to serve the evening meal."

"So did he say it was just him coming back?"

"James said he didn't mention Beth or Willa."

"They've left some of their belongings here. They must be coming back with him."

"We'll find out tomorrow night."

"Tomorrow?" Courtney smiled. Soon she'd see Aaron again.

"Jah, tomorrow."

When Heather's buggy disappeared down the driveway, Courtney closed the door and told the children their father was coming home soon. They hollered and danced around with happiness.

"Just one more sleep?" Amy asked.

"Just one more and he'll be here. Just one more night of me telling you stories and then you'll get your better storyteller back."

"Yeah, *Dat's* better at stories," Jared said.

Courtney was pleased he was coming back not only because she missed him but because she'd been sleeping on the couch in the main house so she'd be closer to the children.

That night Courtney could barely sleep. If he and Willa were now boyfriend and girlfriend she knew she wouldn't be able to stay on. It was clear that Willa didn't like her so there would be no point in staying—and with a wife there would be nothing for her to do around the place.

Then it occurred to her that if Aaron were interested in marrying again he wouldn't have spent so much time, money and effort to build the cabin near his house.

Just as she was finally drifting off to sleep she heard a knock on the door. She pulled her robe on and lit the gas lamp hoping that there wasn't some emergency somewhere. Then she opened the door to see Aaron's smiling face.

She hoped she didn't look dreadful and put her hand to her head. "What are you doing here? I thought you'd be here tomorrow."

"I caught an earlier bus." He took hold of her hand and walked inside.

"Why did you knock?"

"I didn't want to frighten you. Tell me if I'm mad, but I couldn't stop thinking about you all the time I was gone."

"Where are Beth and Willa?"

"They couldn't change their tickets to come back with me, so they're not coming back. I'm sending their things to them."

"Truly?" Her face beamed with delight.

He laughed. *"Jah,* it's true."

Then there was an awkward and   unnatural

silence. There was clearly something he wanted to say and Courtney hoped he was going to propose. If he had been keen on Willa he wouldn't have rushed back to see her. Unless… unless he'd come back to tell her that she had to leave. She put a hand to her stomach. "Come and sit down on the couch."

She moved her pillows and blankets aside so they could both sit. When they were both seated, Courtney took a deep breath. "What is it you want to say to me? It'll be best to say it straight out." She prepared herself to take another disappointment.

"Courtney, will you marry me?"

That was the best thing that he could have said. She looked into his eyes and he smiled back at her.

"Just say 'yes.'"

"Really? You want to marry me?"

"I can't think of anything better."

Courtney looked into the crackling fire. After Mark's death, she didn't think that there'd be another marriage in her life—not that she'd been against another marriage—she hadn't thought anything of it. That was, until she met Aaron. She turned slightly to face him square on. "I can't believe this is all real. I mean, I wasn't sure how you felt."

"I've tried to tell you over the past little while how I felt about you."

"I know, but I thought I might have been reading things into your words."

"Don't string this out on me, Courtney. My heart is racing now."

"Of course. Yes, I will marry you, Aaron."

He pulled her into his arms. "*Denke, denke* for making me so happy. I can't wait to tell the children tomorrow."

"So soon?"

"We're not going to keep this a secret."

"*Nee,* I didn't think we should. It's just that I'll need to get used to the idea."

He laughed. "We can take things slow if you'd prefer, but I'd like us to marry as soon as we can."

Courtney chewed on a fingernail. "Gabriel will have a *vadder.*"

He pulled her finger out of her mouth. "And I'll have another son." Aaron held onto her hand and squeezed it.

"Does Willa know?"

Aaron said, "She will find out tomorrow with everyone else. I didn't tell anyone I was going to ask you in case you said you didn't want to marry me. Now we can tell everyone."

Courtney nodded and kept quiet on her opinion of his sister-in-law.

He looked around him. "You might as well stay here on the lounge tonight. The cabin will be cold without the fire on."

"Are you certain?"

"I'm quite sure. No one's going to spread rumors about us staying under the same roof if it's just tonight and if they do, we're getting married anyway."

Courtney giggled. "That's true. Were there many people at the funeral?"

"There were hundreds there. Bessie had so many friends that I knew there'd be a lot of people there.

I realized while I was there standing over Bessie's grave that life is so short. We're only here for the blink of an eye. That's when I thought 'why wait?' I think we'll make a good pair and we all love Gabriel."

Courtney giggled. "I've already said 'yes.'"

Aaron laughed. "I don't want you to change your mind."

"I won't. I've been fond of you for some time too."

"Fond? We'll have to work on that."

"I wonder what the children will think about us getting married."

"They'll be thrilled. Especially Amy, she's grown so attached to you. Why don't we wake them up now and tell them?"

"Nee! We'll never get them back to sleep." She looked at Aaron to see that he was joking and she giggled again. "I hope they'll be pleased."

"We'll tell them the first thing in the morning."

"Do you want tea or anything?"

"Nee, you go to sleep. I've been on the bus all day and all I want to do right now is sleep." He looked around the room and when he spotted the crib, he walked over and said goodnight to Gabriel even though he was fast asleep. Once he was back next to Courtney who was still sitting on the couch, he leaned over and kissed her on her forehead. *"Gut nacht.* Sleep tight and I'll see you in the morning. Are you warm enough down here?"

"I'm as warm as toast here. *Gut nacht."* Once he was up the stairs, Courtney remade her bed on the couch. Her prayers had been answered and she closed her eyes tightly hoping nothing would happen to stop them from getting married. Everything had been going well until Willa showed up. Was something else like that going to happen? Disappointment was what she'd grown used to in life, but she had to admit she had some things that had gone right.

To stop fears from rushing through her mind, she counted her blessings. Her baby was well and healthy. She'd made a good friend in Heather, and she was happy working for Aaron, and she loved his children. And it had worked out well that Bessie had recommended her for the position in the first place. When she added everything up, she realized that more good had happened in her life lately than bad. To cap it all off, a wonderful man had just proposed to her.

Gabriel had woken up the next morning in time for Courtney to feed him and change him before Aaron woke for breakfast.

When Aaron walked into the kitchen, he said, "Good morning, my future *fraa.*"

Courtney giggled and turned away from the stove to face him. "Good morning. Are you ready to tell the children today?"

"*Jah,* I'm looking forward to it."

"*Gut,* but they'll still be asleep when you leave for work."

"*Nee* they won't. I'm taking the day off. After we take the boys to *schul* we'll see if Amy can stay with Heather. Then we're going to visit the bishop and tell him of our plans."

"We are?"

He nodded.

"You're full of surprises."

"We should get married as soon as possible."

"That suits me just fine." Courtney turned back to the eggs she was cooking, feeling that her past run of bad luck might be well and truly in the past.

They waited until the three children were sitting at the breakfast table.

Jared asked, "Why aren't you at work, *Dat?*"

"Today is a special day. Miss Courtney has agreed to marry me."

Jared and Ben leaped out of their chairs. "We knew it," Jared said.

"I said they would marry," Ben said.

Courtney chewed on a fingernail and looked at Amy who remained silent.

"Do you know what that means, Amy?"

She shook her head.

"When Miss Courtney and I marry she will be your step-*mudder.*"

"You're going to be my *mudder?*"

Courtney nodded and then Amy jumped off her chair and flung her arms around her. "Do I call you *Mamm?*"

"I guess you can. If you want to." Courtney glanced at Aaron to see if that was okay. He gave a small nod. The boys ran to her and hugged her.

"We've got a new *Mamm,*" Ben said.

"I knew it all along," Jared called out.

Courtney laughed with the three children hanging on to her. "It also means you all have another *bruder* in Gabriel."

The two boys cheered and then Amy copied them.

Courtney looked into Aaron's warm brown eyes, and they crinkled at the corners when he smiled at her. Her heart filled with gladness knowing that very soon she would be part of a large proper family just like she'd always wanted.

I cried unto the Lord with my voice,
and he heard me out of his holy hill. Selah.
Psalm 3:4

The End

Thank you for your interest in
'The Pregnant Amish Nanny'
Expectant Amish Widows Book 6

To be first to be notified of
Samantha Price's new releases
subscribe at:
www.samanthapriceauthor.com

Other books in this series:

Book 1

Amish Widow's Hope

Book 2

The Pregnant Amish Widow

Book 3

Amish Widow's Faith

Book 4

Their Son's Amish Baby

Book 5

Amish Widow's Proposal

Samantha Price loves to hear from her readers.
Connect with Samantha at:

samanthaprice333@gmail.com
http://twitter.com/AmishRomance
http://www.samanthapriceauthor.com
http://www.facebook.com/SamanthaPriceAuthor